SAYING GOODBYE

Printed in the United States of America

Cover Design by Adam Murray
amcreative@comcast.net

Disclaimer:

All characters in this book are fictional, from start to finish.

ISBN: 978-1-4507-6261-8

Maurer, Billie Jo, Saying Goodbye

SAYING GOODBYE

BILLIE JO MAURER

Dedication

To my family, who believes in rainbows after the storm.

Foreword

Ecclesiastes 3:1 & 4

To every thing there is a season, and a time to every purpose under the heaven.

A time to weep, and a time to laugh; a time to mourn, and a time to dance.

PROLOGUE - 1994

The hinges screeched their weary objections as Claire pushed through her front door and stepped into the darkened entry hall. Vigorously kicking off her blue leather heels, she felt the unpleasant coldness of the coarse wooden floor seeping up through the soles of her tired feet. She'd just spent an exhausting few hours mingling with many of her unique quilting companions, hugging each one, and speaking her tearful goodbyes. Over the past several years, a lasting bond of friendship had been created among these women as they collectively discovered a sincere love of piecing together a wide variety of fabrics, each stitch calling to mind a personal story that had been shared in the process, and revealing the common threads of their lives.

At long last Claire's life would enter a new season. The Quilt Shop had been sold! Tonight dear friends had flocked to the place of so many poignant memories: memories that would be tucked away in Claire's heart for years to come.

Slowly she made her way to the kitchen, where she slumped onto a chair, crossing one ankle over the opposite knee, and groaning as her hands massaged the tortured extremity. Functioning in these nasty shoes all day was enough to make a cheerful person miserable, and a miserable one downright mean. Her mumbled complaints bounced from wall to wall, echoing in the silence which overshadowed the modest home, and communicating her own long suffering.

The cozy kitchen gave her solace with its cheerful yellow paint, the country scenes which hung in tasteful groupings along the walls, and the white lace curtains that adorned the windows. Sighing deeply, she stood and rescued from the counter-top the empty glass which had been abandoned there the night before. Out of habit she turned on the tap, filled the small container and slowly transferred the water to the two thriving geraniums, whose existence depended not only on her unflagging efforts to keep them well doused, but on their prominent spot on the window sill, where they could soak up the sun.

She smoothed a finger over the dark green foliage, cupped a fragrant bloom in one palm, and murmured, "Someday *I'll* be where I can bask in the sun while someone submerges my soul in unconditional love." Then, pinching off a few yellow leaves, she chuckled to herself. "Great! Now I'm talking to my plants."

Sauntering toward the humming fridge–a nightly habit–she swung the door open to take inventory. There sat the same boring slice of cheese and soft tomato, undoubtedly hanging on throughout the day in hopes that they'd be devoured by sunset. Claire wrinkled her nose. "Sorry, guys, not tonight."

She retrieved a pre-made individual pizza and threw it into the microwave–so much for early preparation to help improve food choices. After all, who could she possibly hope to impress with a size ten figure at this stage of the game? With a shrug she lifted the discarded packaging from the garbage can and glanced at the nutritional breakdown. "How can something so tiny be that fattening?" she groaned aloud.

As she stood leaning against the counter, waiting for her meal to heat, she anticipated another mellow evening on the back porch, working on her project. A yellow sewing box sat poised inside the back door, as if waiting for a friend to sustain. Inside were neatly folded squares of cloth, carefully placed there each night after Clair had diligently and lovingly stitched them together by hand.

She had chosen a design called "Sparkling Stars," the mere mention of which turned her mind back in time to five years before, when she had so boldly visited the hospital maternity ward, unannounced. Claire's eyes misted as the events of that day came so clearly into focus. She had heard from family members that her daughter, who'd left home at the irresponsible age of sixteen, had given birth to a beautiful little black baby: Claire's first granddaughter.

Though uninvited, Claire nevertheless drove to the hospital, where she cautiously made her way to the nursery, longing for a glimpse of the infant. Her tears smudged the viewing window as she pressed her face hard against its surface, willing the partition into nonexistence as she stared into the clear plastic bassinet where the tag read: baby girl 7 lbs 3 oz, name: Star Jonas.

Claire blew wet kisses to the oblivious child, and with eyes closed, could almost smell the sweet aroma of newborn, while she visualized holding a tiny hand and counting toes. But, throughout the succeeding five years, her dream had proved to be just that: a dream. The quilt would be a gift of love for a very special granddaughter, to whom Claire anticipated handing it in person… someday.

The incessant beeping of the timer, indicating that dinner was ready, pulled Claire abruptly from her reverie. Slipping the hot pizza onto a plate and then placing it on top of the sewing box, she pushed open the screen door with her backside, lowered herself into the old unsightly wicker chair, and placed her load onto the floor. Twisting slightly in her seat, she rubbed her hand across the worn fabric of the cushions, where two tattered patches contributed to the pathetic appearance of the sorry piece. "Poor thing," she commented, "you've gone through hell, too."

She lifted a slice of pizza to her mouth and took a small bite. Then, realizing that she wasn't hungry after all, moved the plate to the floor and tugged open the lid of the sewing box, revealing the colorful fabric inside. With needle and thread in hand she picked up where she had left off the night before, and was gradually soothed by the rhythm of her stitches. Within a couple of hours evening shadows appeared through the willow tree beside the porch, and Claire realized that she had managed to survive another day.

The quilt still in her hands, her head nodded, then peacefully fell back against the patchy cushion. "I'll just close my eyes and take it easy for a few minutes," she sighed. Soft calming tears formed in her drowsy eyes as bittersweet recollections infused her thoughts, but not a soul was there to reassure her and wipe them away. "One thing for certain," she pondered, "the choices of the past have brought me to this lonely day."

She felt a sudden chill, or could it have been Samantha there, giving her a spectral hug? Dear, dear Sam; how she missed her stalwart, courageous friend. Her hands began to tremble as memories magnified themselves, playing like a motion picture across the vivid screen of her mind.

CHAPTER 1

It was June 1965, the night of Claire's graduation from the brand new Valley View High School. The principal's face showed traces of sweat as he swiftly gave his closing remarks, congratulating the seniors for being the first class to graduate from this spectacular new school, and reminding them that, as such, they were making history. "Hats off to the Class of 1965!"

Black caps with gold tassels flew into the air, accompanied by roars of jubilation from the triumphant graduates. Parents applauded, students hugged their beloved classmates, and Claire unsuccessfully attempted to locate her high flying cap. Finally shrugging her shoulders in carefree defeat, she navigated her way through the crowd to receive congratulatory embraces from her family. Claire's heart was thumping so hard from the excitement of the day, she had to pause for a minute, and take a deep breath, before continuing on.

She was thrilled to be graduating, but what now? What could possibly be in her future? From the time she'd turned sixteen, she had worked at the Crown Café, which was always packed with the high school crowds. After every school activity, as well as on weekends, this is where everybody who was anybody would meet.

Claire didn't meet, she was the one waiting on all of the other couples, and listening to their chatter. She was thus privy to the greatest and latest news about who had a crush on whom, as well as the smug details the boys would be sharing about their dates, acting as if Claire were deaf!

Claire had many friends, girls and guys, but she wasn't actively dating. On the rare occasions when she was asked out, she would have to check with her mother to see if she could miss work, since her mother counted on her contribution to the family budget and car payment.

Claire now took a second deep breathe, her eyes welling up with tears as she approached her family. Clusters of people were everywhere, awaiting their sons or daughters; some were bearing gifts, while others held bouquets of flowers, but Claire stayed focused on the small group before her.

Her mother Grace, the shortest of the three, was a little stocky, with graying hair, even though she was only in her early forties. She worked as a cook at the Wagon Wheel café, and was known state wide for her pie making. The love of her life had suffered a heart attack at age thirty-five, while working at the Ogden train depot, leaving Grace with two-year-old Claire to raise alone. Up until that time, Ogden had been their home, but after the tragedy, Grandpa Smith packed up his daughter and granddaughter, and took them home with him to Woodland.

Grace had a great friend named Mary, with whom she shared her deepest thoughts and emotions, the two of them sustaining each other through the good times, as well as the bad. Each day Grace would pick Mary up from the Exchange Grocery Store at six o'clock sharp, and the two women would babble about their day as they sipped on a couple of cold Cokes, which Mary would carry out from the grocery store. Grace never remarried and was lonely at times, but she was also very set in her ways, with a lot of pride and determination to take on what fate had dealt her.

Aunt Betty, a couple inches taller than her sister Grace, now shared a smile that warmed Claire through and through. The young graduate lovingly put her arms around her aunt, feelings of gratitude welling up within her for the years of care generously given by this dear woman and her husband during all of the long hours when Grace, out of necessity, had to work. Aunt Betty had four boys of her own, who kept her very busy, but nonetheless had managed to pamper Claire. She'd always seemed to know when the pantry was low, and immediately filled it; or when Claire had special programs, Aunt Betty would appear with a new dress: countless acts of caring and kindness for which Claire would forever be grateful. Because Claire's uncle sold insurance, and traveled world-wide, he was regrettably unable to attend her graduation, but Claire knew that she was nevertheless in his thoughts.

Then there was Grandma: short and stocky, with beautiful white hair, and the deep blue eyes that had been passed down to Claire. Grandma was all in black, with a little feather hanging from her velvet hat, wearing her Sunday dress with the pearl buttons, her black purse with a gold chain clutched tightly in her right hand. She unfailingly wore the same special attire to church on Sunday, and to funerals; now she added Claire's graduation to the list. Claire could see tears in Grandma's eyes, and her bottom lip quivering, and knew that Grandma could feel Grandpa by her side, sharing this special day.

13

As Claire's arms wrapped around Grandma, she felt moisture on her cheek. Cherished were the stories which the older woman had shared over the years, of her own childhood, and how she had fallen in love with Grandpa. She had also related tales of her school experiences, which were distinctly different from Claire's. After all, this younger generation was so disrespectful compared to hers, and now there was this Elvis guy strutting and jiggling on TV. The recollections brought a smile to Claire's lips as she released her grandmother, and whispered "Thank you for coming, Grandma."

Finally, as Claire stood in front of her mother, her facial expression softened. "I love you, Mom. Thanks for all you've done to get me this far, and I promise I will remember to heed your words, and think twice, so I won't make any foolish decisions tonight, and I will drive carefully, and I will not drink, and, and, hmm, have I left anything out?"

"Yes dear, there is a curfew, so don't forget: no later than one o'clock. I get chills, just thinking of you out at that hour, but since I promised I'd let you stretch the rules for graduation…" She shrugged and smiled wryly, putting her arm around Claire as the small group moved slowly out the door, chattering back and forth about the graduation program. Claire fleetingly glanced around, searching for her friends, then turned back to her family.

Aunt Betty reached down and took Claire's hand, slipping her an envelope. "Grandma and I put some money together, Claire, and it will be enough to pay off your car. I checked at the bank, and the balance was 745 dollars."

Claire's mouth dropped open, her squeals drawing attention as she jumped up and down. Then, after suspending her animation long enough to wrap her arms around Aunt Betty and Grandma, and offer a sincere, "Thank you, thank you. I can't believe this!" she squealed and bounced some more!

Between Claire's jumps her mother reached out her hand. "I'll take the envelope so you can go with your friends, and then I have a surprise waiting for you when you get home. Now go and have a nice night, and remember your promises."

As Claire walked across the West parking lot where she was to meet her friends, her heart continued to pound within her. She was actually out of school! What could possibly be waiting for her in the years to come?

Claire always dressed modestly, but had wanted to be a little bit daring when she'd chosen her graduation dress. She had picked a cotton frock with a white skirt and a red and white checked

14

bodice and pockets. She'd been nervous about the shoestring straps, but her mother had approved her choice. Her black hair was pulled back on the sides, and up into a red ribbon. Her skin was a soft creamy white, and her large blue eyes were mesmerizing. She was also very lucky to have inherited a slim body from her father's side of the family, and had all the curves in the right places, but rarely flaunted or exposed herself. She was innocent, yet she liked to flirt. Tonight she felt pretty, and confident, and sassy, but where her atypically carefree attitude would lead her never entered her mind!

Claire's friends were standing by her gray Beatle Bug, and shared hugs before jumping into the vehicle. You could hear their high-pitched screams as the car squealed out of the parking lot. Claire turned on the radio, and they sang–out of tune–as it played, "She Wore Blue Velvet."

Then, spinning the dial to a different station, they bounced to the sounds of rock-n-roll that blurted from the speakers as they continued toward Memorial Hill, about fifteen miles away. The only way to the top was by a narrow road which spiraled upward, and as they made the last turn, sunlight glistened on the huge brass plaque which displayed the names of veterans who had served in several wars.

The group of teens who claimed this area for "hangin' out" were respectful of the memorial, and since it was centered on the south end of the hill, they congregated on the north side. As Claire's car came into view, cheers were heard from the others who were already dancing and celebrating. It didn't take long for Claire and her friends to melt into the familiar crowd.

A few hours later, as the full moon became a backdrop for the Rocky Mountains; a polished, classy, red Chevy Impala convertible cruised slowly into the domain of the celebrating seniors. Voices in the group lowered as they watched the driver make a complete circle around the party, searching for a parking space. The boys were admiring the car, and you could hear sighs coming from the girls, indicating their interest not only in the vehicle, but also in the seven boys who were packed inside.

Robert, who was behind the wheel, caught Claire's eye instantly. As he cruised past, he looked directly at her, giving her tingling shivers up and down her spine. He seemed to have an arrogance about him that made Claire a little jumpy, but, at the same time, she was intrigued by his boldness.

With confidence Robert pulled up next to an old Ford truck, revved the car's motor a couple of times before turning the key off, then moved one hand over the steering wheel, allowing himself a few minutes to ponder his intrusion. A week ago he had convinced his buddies that they could get some action in this hokey little town if they played their cards right. He knew that his sleek new wheels would draw attention, allowing them the access they desired into unknown territory. Once he had laid out the plan, his pals were ready to roll.

The car was a gift from Robert's father, a reward for high performance in football and basketball. Since Mr. Jensen's preoccupation with his business precluded his attendance at Robert's sports events, it might be assumed that the car was perhaps intended as compensation for the perpetually empty seat next to Robert's mother in the bleachers. Between father and son there was no meaningful communication. Mr. Jensen offered no pats on the back, and no verbal praise, only cold remarks as he pecked away at his only child.

Robert was born and raised in Salt Lake City, where his father owned a chain of full service car shops. Robert had graduated from Harrisville High two years earlier, but had not, at that time, been awarded the sports scholarship for which his father had so diligently campaigned. Mr. Jensen held high expectations for his son, but was often disappointed. Nevertheless, he had come through with an unequaled graduation gift: the hot red Chevy Impala convertible. Then, because college had not been an option, Robert's only alternative had been to go to work for his father's company.

His dad had a reputation with the ladies, and his business associates deemed him as an unapproachable tyrant. "Mr. Anthony Jensen" was the way that Robert, with a sarcastic tone, referred to his father. Robert had seen him with many women, being very deceitful to his mother Ella. But the man made money, and bought his friends, as well as his women.

Mr. Jensen enjoyed the social status and the luxury his money provided, and expected Ella to perform accordingly. In public she played the role that was required, nothing less, nothing more. She acted as the perfect wife and hostess to all of his clients, doting on them, and making sure the servants followed her strict instructions with regard to the menu and service. She usually indulged in a few drinks during the parties, to help her relax from the strain of her husband's manipulation. Then, after the entertaining, they went to their separate rooms, as well as their separate lives. Ella was a very lonely woman. She was disgusted with the way she lived her life, but was too weak in her heart to make the changes that would free her from this man. She had mothered Robert the best she could, but there was always the shadow and power of Mr. Anthony Jensen watching over them.

Robert now turned to his friends and said: "Well, Boys, it's time to play ball. Let's be sure we move real slow; we don't want to ruffle any feathers. And, by the way," his voice took on a husky quality, "the pretty brunette with the white dress is mine."

He opened the door and flashed a self-assured, dimpled smile toward the group of guys, then gave his cohorts a wink as they started hoisting cases of beer out of the trunk. Robert noticed that a big percentage of the boys were already holding cans of beer, as they congregated around him and his friends. Robert smiled and said, "My buddies and I wanted to join your celebration!"

The partying crowd looked inquisitively at the car's occupants, and seeing no one that seemed familiar, assumed that they were from Salt Lake City. After all, no one in these parts could afford a car like that! Not waiting for a substantial invitation, the intruders confidently joined the group, their beer being their well accepted calling card.

Claire's deep blue eyes centered on the sexy, self-assured driver of the car, who was obviously trying to get her attention as he nonchalantly leaned back against the fender. With a beer in one hand, he suavely slicked back his hair with the other, riveting his target with a flirtatious expression. Claire, who was unable to keep her intensified focus off of him, zoomed in on his dreamy blue eyes, his profound dimples, his cocky but intriguing attitude, and his self-assurance. Her eyes traveled over his muscular frame and his tight fitting Levi's, then back up to his firm biceps, which were exposed by the rolled-up sleeves of a white T-shirt, finally landing on his incredibly tantalizing smile.

When the radio began playing "Hey, Baby, I wanna know if you'll be my girl," Robert tossed his beer can toward a tree, folded his arms in a self assured way, and mouthed the words of the song slowly toward Claire, then motioned for her to come and dance.

She leisurely approached him, knowing in the pit of her stomach that she was messing with fire. As she cautiously placed her small hand within his rugged one, he drew her slowly toward him, repeating the words of the song in her ear as he held her tight, swaying to the music. The maneuver was corny, but she fell for it. Under that big old moon, with thousands of stars taking the place of lights, and kisses that claimed her innocence, she tumbled for the untamed rebel, thinking the thrill would last forever. They were married a year later.

CHAPTER 2 – 1980

The early morning sun peeped through the colorful fall leaves overhead as Claire bent to the clothes basket on the grass, which was overflowing with freshly washed towels. The two deep pockets on the front of her red apron bulged with wooden clothes pins, the necessary tools for her task. She enjoyed hanging out her wash in the early hours of the morning, before the children started to awaken.

Robert had been up since five; as manager of the local service station, he was expected to be on the job and open for business at six. Claire made sure she had a load of wash in, and Robert's breakfast, which consisted of orange juice, two scrambled eggs, and whole wheat toast, on the table by 5:30 each morning, without fail.

When Robert and Claire married, fourteen years ago, they were completely devoid of wisdom or good sense. Both sets of parents had been troubled over the accelerated rate at which their dating had led to marriage, but the two young people had, early on, disclosed their dedication to each other. Claire's expressed desires were intensified by her tears as she verbalized to Robert her assurance that she would love him forever, and wished for them to have many children together. In return Robert conveyed his everlasting devotion, and declared his determination to be the best that he could be for Claire and their young ones.

Though Robert's ambitions were high, he had settled for his present position with the service station so that Claire could stay in Woodland, close to her family and friends: all that she had ever known. Then, five years after Claire's graduation, her grandmother passed away, leaving a nice inheritance for the surviving daughters. Aunt Betty's husband received a job offer in California that he couldn't resist, and they both exerted themselves in convincing Grace to retire, and move with them to the land of palm trees and sunshine. Claire joined forces, and eventually persuaded her mother to take advantage of the offer, live the dream! She never wanted Grace to know the pain she would experience when she watched the last of her family drive down the lane, and out of sight.

The years had come and gone with each sunrise and sunset, bringing along the desired children: Daniel, Davis, Eliza, Joey and Julie. With the experience Robert had had at his father's shop he was able to do some repairs that added to their income, but the budget was nonetheless tight. Claire worked very hard managing their little family, and, after discovering that she enjoyed working with fabrics, began creating pieced quilt tops for ladies in the area. Her efforts brought in some extra money to help with the necessities, as well as provide for dance lessons and sports activities.

As she stretched up to fasten another towel on the line, she mentally counted her blessings: a handsome and devoted husband, five beautiful children, a comfortable home in a town she loved, and enough money to at least keep the wolf from the door.

Robert, just finishing his breakfast, pushed the kitchen chair back, grabbed his hat from the rack by the back door, and came up behind Claire as she was clipping the last towel to the clothesline. He wrapped his arms around her waist, then gently pressed his lips to the back of her neck. Claire turned within his tight grip to face him, her eyes aglow with the love that bubbled up within her. Robert kissed her possessively, then took a deep breath and released her. "I never get tired of kissing you, Claire." Claire's heart throbbed at his words as she watched him walk to his red Impala, open the door, swivel in under the stirring wheel, and wave goodbye. They were passionately in love, and desired to be together forever and ever.

"Good morning neighbor." Startled by the voice, and embarrassed at the thought of someone watching her intimate moment with her husband, she twirled around, and stooped down to look under the suspended towels in search of the sound.

"My word, George, you startled me. What are you doing up at this time of the morning?"

"I wanted to get a good start on the weeding in the garden. Didn't mean to startle you. What were ya doin' anyhow? All I could see was legs!"

Claire giggled as she made her way under the towels to the white picket fence to visit with her great, but quirky, neighbor. George and Ethel Watson had lived in the house next door for forty-five years: all of their married life. They were both in their late sixties, and the more they worked, the happier they were. Each year George produced an attractive, attention-getting garden, the yield from which he unfailingly shared with the whole neighborhood. His backyard had a sandbox, as well as a tire-swing hanging from the old pipe-dream tree, and in the corner by the garden was a chicken coop, housing fifteen to twenty birds. Claire appreciated the fact that George wanted her children to learn how to care for animals, and included them in his daily chores: feeding and watering his milk cow and chickens, as well as gathering the plentiful eggs, and taking care of special needs when the baby chicks arrived.

Ethel taught piano, but never charged Claire for her girls' lessons. The Watson's hospitality knew no bounds, and the homemade cookies that were always in the cookie jar were just one more manifestation of the couple's unconditional love for their young neighbors.

Because Ethel had had problems with her first pregnancy, their family consisted of only one son, who was married with two children, and living in New York. Therefore, the older couple were ecstatic when Robert and Claire moved in ten years ago. They became instant grandparents, and it didn't take long for Ethel to realize that the love and nurturing thus kindled was essential for both families.

CHAPTER 3

Robert pulled into the station, parking his car on the right side of the building, where the large windows would allow him to keep an eye on it while he sat inside at his desk. Robert still got a kick out of driving the convertible, which it was his pleasure to keep in mint condition.

He walked around to the front, turned the key in the lock, flipped on the lights, and proceeded with the daily routine of preparing the station for customers. He had worked hard to establish a clientele who returned on a regular basis for gas, tune ups, and major overhauls when required. He was honest in his dealings, as well as patient with those who needed extra attention, due to the nature of their vehicle's problems.

Robert had leased the station from Mr. Morris, a native of Woodland who'd been anxious to retire. The business had been in his family for years, and he'd wanted someone who would continue to practice the high standards set in place by the original "Morris & Sons." Robert was the guy who'd been chosen from all the applicants to meet this challenge. Robert's intentions were sincere when he accepted the job, and he felt a strong obligation to Mr. Morris for giving him this opportunity. In the back of his mind he also wanted to prove to his father that he could make it on his own.

Robert was lining up the worksheets as Rex, his only employee, entered the front door. Rex was an achiever, hard working and honest. He was twenty-five, and had recently become a first time father, when his wife presented him with a son, Andy. In the five years that Rex had been with the station, he'd never missed a day on the job. He and Robert, both, had put their work ethics together in building up the business.

Rex picked up his worksheets and went directly to the parts room, where he gathered the items on the sheets, and then headed out to the work area. Pressing the red button that lifted the outside door, he saw that three cars were already lined up for their appointments. Rex smiled, and motioned with his hand for them to pull into their designated bays.

Robert, still in his office, heard the bell ring out front, indicating that a car had pulled up for gas. He hurried outside, recognizing, as he went, one of his regular customers: the only woman he knew with pink hair, and, of course, the accompanying nickname. He'd always wondered which had come first: the moniker or the startling tresses. Walking quickly around to the driver's door, he flashed Pinky a dimpled smile, as she rolled down her window, and greeted him with a bat of her false eyelashes. "Hi handsome; I always like starting my day with the looks of you, and if you were twenty years older, I'd be a little more flirty."

"You must be working the morning shift, Pinky," he observed as he shoved the gasoline nozzle into her tank, and began washing the windshield. "Do you want me to fill up the old Ford?"

"Yeah, and yeah. The boss has given me straight mornings from now on. He said I make the best coffee, and the customers complain when Holly is there instead. I don't know if that's a compliment or not, but I took it as one."

Robert finished polishing the windshield, and threw the rag into the bucket by the front door. He then topped off the tank, returned the hose to the pump, and sidled up to the driver's side window. "Okay, Sweetie, you're good to go; that will be fifteen even."

She dug three fives from her pocketbook, and handed them to him. "Tell Claire 'hello,' and give those cute kids a hug from Pinky," she said with a wink, as she drove away.

Robert could hear the phone ringing, and, knowing that Rex was busy with repairs, he quickened his steps as he crossed through the open doorway, then reached over the counter to pick up the black receiver.

"Good morning; Morris & Son's. This Robert Jensen. What can I do to help you?"

"Robert, this is Randy. Remember me, Buddy?"

"Randy! Wow! I haven't heard from you since we graduated. What's up?"

"Well, good things I hope, and depending on this phone call, it could get a lot better."

He proceeded to fill Robert in on the purpose of his call. Since their graduation in 1963, Randy had been working side by side with his father, who had just recently passed away in a bad automobile accident in Colorado. Now he was looking for someone whom he could trust, who was dependable, and who would help him build up the business. Randy was asking Robert to be that person. Robert naturally had a lot of questions, and, for once, was thankful that no customers

22

pulled up for gas during the next thirty minutes.

As he slowly lowered the receiver back to its base, he took a deep breath, running his hand through his thick black hair. Was he dreaming this? Randy had just offered him a job as a supervisor in Colorado, where he would be managing a warehouse that distributes car parts nationwide. Randy also wanted to expand the business, erecting warehouses in California and Nevada, and he wanted Robert to oversee those projects from start to finish. The money offered was ten times what he was now making. Granted, he would be working more hours, and spending the majority of his time away from home, but once he was established, he could move Claire and the kids to Colorado.

He couldn't pass this up; his buddy had come out of nowhere, offering him a new life. Robert's heart was beating fast, as visions of unlimited success energized his mind. Money! Money could buy them a new home, a new car, a whole new way of living. Claire could have more of the things she deserved. It wasn't that they didn't have a good life, but Robert believed this would be their yellow brick road to happiness.

CHAPTER 4

"You want to do what?" Claire's voice resounded throughout the back yard. Robert sat beside her, posed on the outdoor swing that claimed its place on the rock patio. The old apple tree, which provided a bulwark for the children's tree-house, cast its shade from the west side of the area, and Claire could still hear the echo of childish laughter and shouts, as Robert helped them nail the old boards to the tree. George had provided the lumber from his barn, and one plank had a knothole in it that made a perfect lookout for intruders.

The family spent many enjoyable hours here in their yard, hosting neighborhood gatherings, as well as numerous birthday parties. Claire especially loved the fire pit, over which they roasted marshmallows and hot dogs. She had mixed emotions, however, about the tree. When her oldest son Daniel was six, he had climbed into its branches while playing pirates with the neighbor's boy. His subsequent, and possibly predictable, fall had resulted in a broken arm. As Claire and Robert rushed him to the hospital, she suffered severe emotional trauma, and asked Robert to chop the thing down. But the tree still stood, with leafy branches that whispered many stories.

"How long will you be gone? Why would you even entertain the idea of such a massive change? Who will help me with all the boys' sports, let alone the outdoor chores? Robert, I know the money sounds generous, but our family will be torn apart! Is this what you really want?" Claire's voice rambled on as the sun set behind the apple tree, casting long shadows across the lawn. Thank heavens the children had gone with George to get feed for the chickens.

"Claire, will you listen to me! The separation will only be for a few months, and I'll be able to fly home on some of the weekends. I know it's going to be rough for awhile, but it will all be worth it once I get the other two warehouses up and running. We'll have doors open that will bring us an exceptional lifestyle. The children will have amazing opportunities for their education."

"What about the lease on the station?"

Robert draped his arm around her shoulders. "Rex is going to take over the lease; this has also opened a door for him and his family. Trust me, Claire. Be strong, and back me up on this, will ya, Hon?"

Claire's heart and mind were sending her warnings that frightened her. She didn't have all of the answers; she wanted to support Robert, but it just didn't seem right. She was sure that many women felt like this as their husbands left to fill positions in the military, but this wasn't a call to duty, it was a fly-by-night offer from a so-called friend that Robert hadn't seen, or heard from, in years. Now he wanted to drop everything, and follow the elusive dream. Maybe Claire needed to calm down, and trust him; after all, his mind was made up. He wasn't asking for permission; he was dominating her, which added to her cause for worry. Where would this path lead?

Claire sighed, and looked at her husband. "You're not seeking my approval, Robert. Your mind was made up long before you approached me. I have many concerns, and the children will be devastated, but I don't think we really have the option to say no."

One month later Robert boarded a plane for Colorado. It was a cold October day as the children lined up by the window at the airport, and watched their dad disappear into the sky. Claire wiped the tears from their cheeks, knowing in her heart that their life would never be the same. She prayed that Robert had made the right decision, not just for him, but for the family.

CHAPTER 5

Following her usual morning routine, Claire reached down into the clothes basket, picking up the last towel to clip to the line. It was a beautiful fall day, the leaves once again presenting a colorful display which Claire never tired of. She missed the passionate embrace that she'd been in the habit of receiving, each morning, before Robert maneuvered his way toward his prized car to go to work. Sighing deeply, she wiped away a tear that traveled slowly down her cheek.

"Well, little woman, what ya doin today?" George leaned on the fence with one hand, while the other held a large rake. "I can't see yer head, but I can see yer feet, so I know yer there."

Claire parted two of the towels, and peeped through the opening. "George, you illuminate my life; did you know that? I can be engaged in a struggle with my thoughts and emotions, feeling unhopeful, as well as frumpy, and your voice alone pulls me back to the day, to the minute, endorsing the purpose of my existence. So, the answer to your question is: I'm washing, baking cookies for Daniel's scouting fund raiser, running Davis and Joey to the barber for haircuts, and taking Eliza and Julie for ice cream, provided they're respectful to their brothers today."

"Holy moley, girl, ya gotta give me some time with 'em. I want 'em to help me rake up the leaves, and bag 'em, and I expect they'll want a period of play before we're through. I know, when I was a pup of a boy, my dad made sure we dallied a bit before the hard work began.

"How bout you take Davis and Joey for haircuts, and give me the rest of em? Mom's just got done with a batch of raisin filled cookies; we'll put em on a nice plate, and you can take 'em for the bake sale. That way ya might have some time for yourself."

Claire winked at George, nodding her head in approval. She picked up the basket, did a quick check of her dying flower beds, then opened the back screen door, and went inside, mentally thanking God for George and Ethel.

Claire and Robert had always taken the children to church on Sunday, and were faithful in holding family prayers each evening. Family nights, though interspersed with the usual fights between the children, also introduced goals for them to work on, and afforded them time to express their love for one another. Now it was up to Claire, alone, to make sure they continued attending church, and participating in family night. It was lonely without Robert there, but they always called him to include him in the prayers, by assigning one child each week to hold the phone out so Dad could hear them pray.

Just as Robert had promised, there was now more money for the family's support. Claire continued piecing quilts, but for a hobby now, instead of a necessity. His company had opened a new distribution warehouse in San Diego just a year after Robert hired on, but after an additional twelve months, the kickoff for the Nevada project was still a ways off. Robert was forever flying back and forth, but felt that Claire and the children were better off staying in familiar surroundings, so he never encouraged the idea of the family relocating to Colorado.

He failed to perceive how much he was missing, as the children grew up without him. The boys, especially, yearned for their dad to attend their baseball and football games. Bless George; he yelled louder than any parent on the bench, then praised, as well as rewarded, the young athletes for good sportsmanship, and honest efforts in the games. While George was becoming their hero, Robert seemed to be just a voice on the phone line, with a lot of empty promises.

The sun was setting behind Mt. Timpanogos, as the last little league football game of the season ended in defeat for the struggling Wasps. Claire loaded the boys into the car, listening to them argue the reasons for Davis's team losing the game. Daniel, being two years older, had all the answers, putting blame on the referees' stupid calls, but Davis didn't want to hear it.

"George said it's just a game, Daniel, so chill out."

George and Ethel approached Claire's car. "How about I treat ya all to some ice cream up at the Crown?" Cheers could be heard from the boys, and shrieks from the girls, as they clapped their approval of George's suggestion.

Claire slowly followed the Watsons as they drove out of the park, and onto the old back road that lead to Main Street. Judging from the traffic, everyone else had the same idea. The Crown was still the place to eat, have ice cream, and just hang out.

Once they found a parking place, Daniel helped Davis put his football gear into the trunk of the car, then they ran toward George and Ethel who were holding the door open for them. Claire and the girls skipped together for a few steps, smiling at their generous neighbors as they entered the Café.

The children's eyes were temporarily glued to the ice cream glass, while they tried to decide on their favorite flavors. Miss Peggy, the owner's daughter, was doing the scooping, her white apron smeared with many colors of ice cream: a testimonial to her hard work. She was a tall thin woman, who wore her salt and pepper hair in a bun at the top of her head, and kind of reminded Claire of the wicked witch in the *Wizard of Oz*, though her temperament was more like Glinda's. She had never married, so still lived at home with her parents, who now needed her help in caring for them.

Miss Peggy was one of those people who knew everything, and then some, about what was going on in town. She was now chattering away to one of the customers about a soon-to-be-opened quilt shop. The new owners were renovating Mrs. Murray's dress shop on the corner, and would be offering sewing classes, with an emphasis on quilting. Miss Peggy's voice was high pitched as she expressed her excitement over the Crown Café's close proximity to the new business. "I hope they can teach an old fogey like me a few new tricks," she said as her head swivelled around in Claire's direction.

"Oh, hi there, George, Ethel. Didn't see ya standin there, but I do see some weird lookin' faces attached to the ice cream glass."

"Uh, that couldn't be my kids, Miss Peggy," asserted Claire. "You must be seeing aliens; my kids are so well behaved, they wouldn't dream of pressing their noses to the glass."

They all shared a chuckle, and then, one by one, ordered their favorite flavors. George motioned them to come over to the round table he had secured in the midst of all the customers, where, after each had claimed a chair, they chatted back and forth about the day's events.

Claire leaned across the table so Ethel could hear her words above the competing prattle of the large crowd that was still lingering. "I'm really interested in the quilt classes; would you like to go?"

Ethel also leaned forward to reply, "I don't think so, Claire; I have a big box in my closet, full of projects I've never finished. But why don't you go, and we'll watch the children." George smiled at her suggestion, and Claire was grateful that she could have a night out, just to do something that she loved.

CHAPTER 6

A crooked line formed from the front door, down the sidewalk, to the corner. As the women worked themselves up the street, they were greeted along the way with a variety of quilts positioned on the white picket fence that separated them from the storefront. The sandstone building had once been the home of long-time resident Mr. Buell. When he passed on, Mrs. Murray purchased the house, straightaway knocking out some walls to make one big room, so she could display her dresses and accessories in a cheery fashion.

Mrs. Murray had a reasonably steady clientele, but, after being a widow for so many years, she could not ignore the suit of a charming man, who often stopped in town on his way to do some fly fishing in the near-by Jordan River. They initially met in a coffee shop, and it wasn't long before the relationship blossomed to the point that Mrs. Murray closed her shop, and drove away with the new love of her life.

Gertrude Barnes, for many years involved with fabric shops as a customer, all the while dreaming of someday acquiring her own, was now following her aspiration as the proud, and awe-inspiring, owner of "A Stitch in Time." The newly remodeled shop faced the town's main street, and the creatively decorated white picket fence, which danced around the entire property, made it very easy to lure in the customers.

On this, the opening day of business, Miss Peggy was the first one to line up in front of the old wooden door, currently embellished with a straw wreath (the door, not Miss Peggy), cleverly displaying all kinds of notions for quilting. At ten o'clock, sharp, the door was flung open, and there stood Gertrude, smiling from ear to ear, as the ladies squealed in delight.

Claire patiently worked her way to the threshold, and stepped inside. Instantly the fragrance of lilac trees filled her nostrils, the pleasant scent coming from numerous jar candles, burning around the room, and releasing their redolent aroma. She turned to the right where, in place of the original front windows of the home, was a little alcove full of displays, boasting the talents of those who would be teaching the classes. Claire could hear the high pitched voice of Miss Peggy chattering away, and smiled to herself, sympathizing with the unfortunate victim of the friendly onslaught, and hoping that, whoever it was would be able to break away.

Claire was drawn to the exhibit that read: ***Creative Nine Patch by Samantha Rose Parker***, where miniature nine patch squares had been sewn together to make a beautiful table runner. On one side was a puffy pillow with a nine patch pattern made from Christmas fabrics, and, on the other, several different pieced quilts were attractively arranged over the back of a chair. Clair was intrigued by the display, and fascinated by the labor of love the teacher had exhibited.

A pleasant voice interrupted her thoughts, and she elevated her eyes, forcing them to leave the intriguing array, as she turned. There stood a captivating, small framed lady, the same height as Claire, and appearing to be about the same age. Her eyes were a soft faint blue, almost misty, and her silky black hair was pulled up into a perky pony tail. A few freckles gave added charm as they danced across her nose. Claire was spellbound by her soft smile. The woman wore casual black slacks, and a simple white blouse, with a vest made of miniature pieced fabric squares, hand stitched together, with the meticulous stitching on the topside. The finishing touch was the antique buttons skipping from top to bottom.

"Is this your display?" Claire's words were spoken with virtual reverence.

"It is, and I would love to teach you the techniques."

There were just a few minutes of silence, as the two ladies perceived one another's spirits. They were drawn together, feeling a precognitive familiarity, one with the other, something akin to a sacred bond.

Miss Peggy's shrieking voice broke the silence as she put her arm around Claire's shoulders, and burst out formal introductions. "Claire, this is Samantha; Samantha, this is Claire."

Simultaneously the two women reached out and locked hands, saying together, "It's nice to meet you." If Miss Peggy had been psychic, her introduction would have gone more like this: "Claire and Samantha, I hereby pronounce you kindred spirits, till death do you part!"

Hours later Claire was writing out a check for 175 dollars, payable to "A Stitch in Time." As she signed at the bottom, she had a passing thought, wondering if Robert ever checked on the amounts, and recipients, of her expenditures. He had never given her a so-called budget, but she still tried very hard to put limits on her purchases, endeavoring to distinguish between wants and needs. This purchase was definitely a great big want! She was planning to surprise Robert with a nine patch quilt for the four poster bed that they shared. With the gifted teaching talents that Sam would provide (*Samantha requested the shorter version of her name*), Claire was sure she could accomplish her goal, and hopefully, when Robert came to visit again, the two of them would be lying upon the beautiful covering together.

CHAPTER 7

Robert held his pencil between two fingers and repeatedly tapped it on the desk. His mind was dancing here and there, back and forth, with thoughts–oddly enough–about his father. He had cause to worry that he was becoming the man he loathed. For example: he didn't mind being away from his family for long periods of time; he reveled in his work, and the sense of great power it gave him. He enjoyed conquering the obstacles and challenges inherent to the expansion of the company's product and work force.

Denver was nothing like he had expected, picturing cold winters and hot summers. The winters were actually quite mild, and the summers were cool and comfortable. Robert mused over Denver's long and priceless history, beginning as a little town in the middle of nowhere. The story went that, as angels were carrying the city to its proper place, they accidently dropped it in the midst of a wilderness. From that ignominious beginning, the divinely abandoned little village had struggled; its inhabitants scrambling to keep it alive. Robert found it interesting that Colorado, at that time, had more ghost towns than live ones, 500 to be exact.

His office was in the heart of the city, by Union Station, and when he wasn't there, he was flying to San Diego, where he was heavily involved in the operation of the new distribution center. Though, awhile back, he wouldn't have thought it possible, being diverted from his family for months at a time was becoming an acceptable lifestyle for him. And isn't that what he despised most about his father? Claire seemed to be getting accustomed to their way of life, but the children were wisely selective in offering their love and allegiance, and it was not Robert, but George, who was the benefactor.

Though Robert had been determined that he would not become like his father, given the circumstances, it was difficult not to slip comfortably into his parent's shoes. Nevertheless, he was fighting it, and in that spirit began to formulate plans for a two week Christmas holiday with his family. He would surprise them with numerous gifts, not the least of which would be a week's stay at a chalet in Park City, so they could take skiing lessons. He became exhilarated as the idea ran rapidly around in his mind; this would bring back all the love of his family, full circle.

Anxious to share his thoughts with Claire, he checked the time on his watch, 7:00 p.m., then picked up the phone and called home. No answer. Three rings, four, seven; where could she possibility be at this time of the evening? His mind did a mental check. Thursday was a school night; she should be home right now, helping the children with homework, but still no answer!

As Robert attempted to replace the receiver, it slipped out of his hand, and crashed into the picture of Claire and the children, knocking it to the floor, and shattering the glass into small insignificant pieces. Swearwords flowed spontaneously from his mouth, cursing his own clumsiness with such an easy task as hanging up the phone. In frustration he retrieved the broom from his office closet, and was in the process of sweeping up the glass, and depositing it into the small trash can by his desk, when Steve, one of his co-workers, poked his head through the door.

"Are you coming?" Steve yelled out. "It's time to drown our sorrows, Buddy."

Robert had a first-rate working relationship with his all-important colleagues. They were a good group of guys, in his estimation, and he enjoyed issuing challenges to them in the work environment. They all exerted a good deal of effort in figuring out what was best for the company, theorizing together about the most profitable alternatives so the business could continue to grow, and receiving generous paychecks for their endeavors.

Robert grabbed his leather jacket, and dashed through his office door to the elevator, where the rest of the guys had assembled. As the glass incased lift made its way to the bottom floor, they could see the skyline of Denver and the top of Union Station. The smell of rain was lingering in the air as they walked around the corner to the Last Stop Bar.

Robert looked forward to having a few drinks at the end of a working day: a weekly, guilty indulgence that he wasn't about to reveal to Claire. To his dismay, with that thought came instant recognition of another similarity between his own behavior and that of his father. As he took a seat at the pub table, he didn't experience his typical high spirits. Perhaps it was his ongoing reflections, along with his earlier awkwardness with the phone, that were whittling away at him, leaving him hammered and restless. He was trying to pinpoint the exact cause of his anxiety when, to his surprise, as well as that of his cohorts, an attractive waitress immediately began arranging drinks in front of them.

"The bar-tender said to bring you boys the usual; have I got it right?"

She moved from her position on the other side of the table, to stand next to Robert, her leg pressing firmly against his thigh. He glanced up, gazing into hazel eyes, his acceptance of her advances plainly apparent. She was a very attractive blonde, with a provocative manner, and curves that never ended. Robert took the pleasure of scanning her body as he sipped his drink.

"Does the drink meet your expectations?" she drawled seductively.

Robert again made eye contact. "The drink surpasses anything I've tasted for along time. Are you new here? I don't believe I've seen you around."

The corners of her inviting lips curled upward. "Maybe you need to come around more often."

Her naturally blonde hair fell forward as she leaned over the table, tantalizing the men while distributing napkins, and secretly relishing their lewd gawks at the unrestricted view afforded by her low-cut blouse.

Robert's heart quickened at the images his mind was conjuring up, and he took pleasure from the burning in the pit of his stomach. Shelly's obvious eagerness to please him brought facetious whines from the others, and demands for a little more service at their end of the table. She merely winked and walked away, while Robert's buddies smirked knowingly.

Steve gave a low whistle. "Now that's what I call a sweet dream, especially for a lonely married guy."

Yeah, Robert thought, *a guy can certainly let his imagination run wild.* An involuntary response instantly flew through his mind like a witch on a broom: *welcome to your dad's world*!

Claire tucked each child into bed after listening to their touching prayers. She'd never been able to comprehend how one heart could hold so much love. Returning to her bedroom, she glanced at the quilt top lying on her bed, admiring the piece work that Sam had so patiently continued to teach her during each Thursday night class. She hoped that Robert would appreciate the time consuming stitches that held together this work of art, her unconditional gift of love. Running her hand fondly across the fabric, she whispered softly, "I love you passionately, Robert. Wherever you are tonight, I pray you're safe."

CHAPTER 8

Claire kneeled on the Victorian couch that occupied the spot in front of the large bay window in her living room. Her soft hands parted the lace curtains as she watched the wet snow flakes dance to the ground. It was a peaceful sight, a silent offering of serenity.

Soon now Robert would be pulling up in the car he'd rented from the airport, and she was like a giddy schoolgirl waiting for her first date to arrive, with butterflies churning in her tummy. Silly thoughts for someone who had been married for fifteen years. But with Robert coming and going for the last three of those years, it felt like an honor each time he returned home.

She and the children missed him terribly; her heart ached, knowing all the little memories he was missing. But it was their crazy way of life now, and she had to have faith in this alternative lifestyle. She depended on George as a father figure, and, as such, he surpassed all expectations. She sometimes retrieved all the memories George was providing for the children, and ran them through her mind as if they were a movie, wondering in her heart if Robert would have felt the same deep affection and patience for his children that George did, on a daily basis.

She had been up since 4:30 a.m., making homemade cinnamon rolls for breakfast, and seeing to it that all of their bags were packed. More importantly, she wanted to look nice for Robert, so she took a long soothing bath in fragrant oils, and made sure her hair glimmered as it fell to her shoulders. She also took great pains with her makeup; it had to be just right, showcasing her big vivid dark-blue eyes. Claire figured the children would awaken around eight, just about the time that Robert would be arriving, so cinnamon rolls and fruit seemed the way to go. They could then have a hearty lunch after they arrived and got settled at the Park City resort, two hours away.

A week ago Robert had sent a huge box to the family via UPS. The children had squealed in delight upon its delivery, their efforts to rip it open together soon converting into an impatient tug of war. When they finally succeeded in exposing the contents, they found knitted hoods, gloves and scarves to match, with an enclosed note which read:

Merry Christmas! We are going to spend two weeks together skiing, and making snowmen in
Park City. See you soon.
Love, Daddy.
P.S. I let Santa know where he could find us.

Claire's eyes had filled with tears, watching her children jump up and down as they tried to discover which hat fit whom.

Now the day had finally arrived, and Claire and the children were anxiously waiting for Daddy. She missed him. As the car pulled into the driveway, she stepped onto the porch, pulling the sleeves of her sweater down to cover her hands, and hugging herself against the chill of the cold wet snow.

Robert opened the car door, and looked at Claire, that same rush he had felt so many years ago coming back to him. Oh, how he loved this woman, standing on the porch, quivering from the weather, as a shower of snowflakes skittered around her. Robert closed the car door, his steps making footprints in the snow as he started walking toward his wife. The closer he came, the more he knew, in his heart, that his flirtation with the waitress Shelly was just for amusement. This attractive woman on the porch was his soul-mate, as well as the mother of his five children, and he would always feel a deep and abiding affection for her.

Robert took the four steps to the top of the porch, and wrapped his arms tightly around Claire, gazing into her glistering blue eyes as he slowly leaned his head toward her, and very softly kissed her lips. He was home: home with his heart; home with his soul.

He then took off his jacket, and wrapped it around her shoulders, protecting her from the elements, while he reached forward and opened the front door, continually kissing her as they stepped together into the house. Claire broke away from him long enough to take his coat and hang it in the hall closet, while Robert, taking a deep breath, announced, "I have a surprise for you and the children."

Claire couldn't imagine what more there could be; this trip to Park City for Christmas had had them reeling for weeks. When she gave him a questioning look, his brow was lowered and his face displayed a teasing smirk.

"What could you possibly add to this great holiday?" she asked, walking toward him.

"I also invited George and Ethel to go with us. I reserved a very nice cabin right next to our lodge. I wanted to do something pleasant for them; I guess it's my humble way of saying 'thank you' for being here for my family."

"Did they accept?"

"Heck, yes! They'd been all bummed out because they had no one to share Christmas with, since I was taking 'their family' to Park City. So, they are all packed and ready to go. Plus, I arranged for a limo, so we could all go together, and not worry about the drive."

Tears instantly traveled down Claire's cheek. "Now see what you've done; you've ruined my makeup," she whimpered. She was so touched by Robert's sensitivity toward George and Ethel that it was hard to hold back her emotions.

Robert sauntered closer and whispered in her ear, "Let me kiss those tears away, and then we'll go wake up our family, and start this crazy adventure."

The limo arrived right on time, the suitcases stood, ready, by the door, but the children were clustered around their father, mesmerized by his presence. Daniel, fifteen, was almost as tall as Robert, as they stood, side by side, listening to thirteen year old Davis, whose narrative was detailing an elaborate description of how George had helped him earn his scouting badges, instilling in him a desire to continue with the program, so he could someday earn his Eagle award. Daniel wasn't as interested in scouting as Davis and nine-year-old Joey were; he was totally drawn to restoring old cars. George had an old Model "T" Ford in his garage, and he was helping the young man learn the patience required in refurbishing a prized relic.

George now maintained a position on the other side of Robert, listening to the boys, thankful that Robert couldn't see the tears well up in his eyes. But, just then, Robert turned, and looked straight at him, his voice humble as he said, "I wish I'd had a dad like George. And I'm thankful you boys have a praiseworthy man like him right next door; he is our hero."

Eliza and Julie were concentrating on placing little fur coats on their brand new Barbie dolls, a pre-Santa gift that Daddy had given them. Robert would never have thought about Barbies, if he hadn't mentioned his plans to Shelly one night in the pub. She said little girls always love dolls, especially that particular one. So he took her advice, and made a purchase in the airport before he flew out of Colorado. The rest of the Christmas gifts he'd had shipped to the lodge for Santa to pick up.

"Well," said Robert, "our limo is waiting; let's go have some fun."

George, a huge grin splitting his face, hugged Ethel with one arm, and held the front door open with the other, while everyone breezed through. Though the squeals from the girls were a bit much, his joy outweighed the painful sensation in his ears.

CHAPTER 9

As Claire, Robert, George and Ethel huddled together on the back bench of the horse drawn sleigh, they could hear the children's giggles of anticipation filtering back toward them. The two Clydesdale horses snorted, and shook their heads impatiently, waiting for the driver to check the sleigh, and distribute extra blankets to its occupants. Clydesdales are known for their large frames and sturdy working abilities, so pulling the sleigh over the snow covered road would be a fairly easy task for them.

The coachman finally hopped up onto the wooden seat, and picked up the reins. At his command of, "Let's go boys," the horses' powerful first steps caused the passengers in the sleigh to respond with awe, along with more giggles from the girls.

Robert was feeling a bit sentimental, knowing that this was the last day of their Christmas fantasy. He sensed that this fairytale holiday would be a memory that remained in everyone's hearts, forever and ever. His mind strayed back over the past few days, conjuring up images of himself skiing with all three of his boys. They'd had first-class instructors, some of whom followed behind, while others guided them from up front.

George, Ethel, Claire and the girls had shopped while Robert and the boys skied. Like Daniel said, "This is a man's thing." Not that George wasn't a man, but he had, nevertheless, opted to monitor the shopping spree.

Then there was the afternoon when everyone else was busy playing board games by the glowing fireplace inside, and Robert took the girls to make snow angels in the area behind their lodge. They had put on their snow pants, coats, gloves and knitted hats, and Robert had lain on his back in the deep cold snow, Eliza on his right side, and Julie on his left. As they moved their arms back and forth, making the angel wings, Eliza sighed, and in a loud voice, said, "I love you Daddy." From the prominent snow covered hills behind them the tender endearment echoed back, then echoed once more. It was as if an angel were sitting on top of the mountain, breathing in Eliza's words, and fondly returning them, double-fold.

Robert thought he might shatter from the heavy thumping inside his chest, as he slowly drawled a sincere, "And I love you right back." A genuine tear rolled down his cheek, on the side of his face that was next to Julie.

Noticing her father's emotion, she jumped up, saying, "Daddy, I know what makes tears ago away." Robert tried to respond, but the words wouldn't come. Julie then lay upon his chest and said, "Butterfly kisses. I will give you butterfly kisses, Daddy, so your tears will fly away." Robert was overcome with love for all of his children, but most especially, at that moment, for this little daughter, who did, indeed, banish his tears with her magical kisses.

In the middle of the week, the family also participated in a snowman mania, searching for anything and everything that could be used to adorn their frigid friends. Before George and Ethel came outside to join them, the group huddled together, and decided to make a George snowman, and a Ethel snow-woman. As the Watsons sauntered out of their cabin door, the children grabbed chairs from inside, placed them by the outdoor heater on the porch, and escorted the pair to their places of honor. "We want to surprise you," they chanted.

The family worked hard and fast, rolling huge snow balls to mount, one on top of the other. When they were close to the end result, Claire covered George's eyes, and Robert covered Ethel's, while the children, without delay, dressed the snow people: one in George's hat and red flannel shirt, the other gussied up with Ethel's long apron, and hair net, her slippers being placed in their appropriate positions at the bottom of the sculpture. Then, amid much laughter from the unsuspecting couple, and in turn, from the whole family, they all went into the lodge to pop popcorn, and enjoy some old time root beer, the label on which read *Dad's*.

As the sleigh finished its tour, and pulled up in front of the lodge, the driver jumped down to assist the adults in alighting from their seats. The children had, one by one, nodded off as they came back down the canyon, and were now sleeping peacefully. Robert gently nudged Daniel and Davis, who awoke, stretched, and headed toward the lodge, groggily wobbling up the path toward the door. George took hold of Joey, and Ethel surrounded Eliza with her arms, as Robert lifted the still slumbering Julie, and they all walked very carefully up the snowy path, and through the door.

Within the hour all the children had on their pajamas, and were tucked into bed. George approached Robert, and with cracking voice, thanked him for a wonderful Christmas. "The gifts were fantastic, Robert, and you put so much planning into this trip. Ethel and I can never thank you enough, but the most precious gifts of all were the memories we made as a family." He patted Robert on the back, while Ethel kissed his cheek. Claire was taken by the deep affection that filled the room. George and Ethel then blew her a kiss, and walked out the door to go to their cabin.

"Well, Lady Love, it's just you and me." Robert took Claire gently into his arms, and said, "I want to share some butterfly kisses with you. I had a great teacher." He leaned forward, and whispered softly, "Close your eyes as I kiss your tears away."

They walked into the sleeping room, where Robert waited while Claire went to the powder room to get ready for bed. As she changed into her nightie, she could hear soft music playing. With her hand lightly on the knob, she slowly opened the door. Their room was dark, except for the glowing candles placed on the night stands and dresser. The scent captivated Claire, and she timidly glanced toward Robert. He stood with his shirt off, revealing his muscular frame, his hand stretched out to Claire. "May I have this dance?'

She walked languidly toward Robert's open arms, and fell into his embrace. As they danced cheek to cheek, Robert sang the words that were filling the room: the same song they had danced to sixteen years ago. They swayed, kissed without interruption, and they loved.

CHAPTER 10

Claire walked into the bedroom and stood in front of the full length mirror, accessing the image reflected there. She turned to the right, then to the left, summing up the quality of her figure. Thirty-six years old, hmm; she stared intensely, searching deeply within herself. Her best features were her enormous blue eyes, which she used to bewitch those in conversation with her, especially if they were meeting for the first time. Depending on the day, she could be charming, approachable, congenial, looney, humble, boisterous, spiritual, a super-mom, a lover, uncomplaining, nagging, or lonely.

She passionately loved being a mother, and was pretty even tempered when it came to parenting the children. Robert, on the other hand, became agitated when things didn't go smoothly. And now, to make things worse, his priorities were not focused on being a full-time father, and a great provider; he had become a fly-by-the-seat-of-your-pants dad. He was more of a stand-by dad. *Oooh, that hurt.* She shook her finger at her image in the mirror. All of the "Dad" credit certainly went to George. "Bless his heart," she murmured softly. This whole arrangement would be a disaster without him.

Claire pulled her thick black locks up into a pony tail, reaching her arm toward the top of the dresser for a rubber band. She liked her hair that way; it took the weight off of her neck, and, with jeans and t-shirt, gave her a get-up-and-go attitude. Suddenly her mind envisioned a different image in the mirror. She was elegantly attired in an attractive red dress, with tiny white rose buds adorning the neckline: the outfit she had purchased for the Valentine's Dance, not too far away. She hoped it would accomplish its purpose: to take Robert's breath away. "My, my," she said to herself, "aren't we having fun with the reflection in the mirror this evening? But we'd better get back to the down-to-earth here and now, or we'll be late for our quilting class."

"Just one more thing," she voiced to herself, as she leaned over her makeup bag, situated on the floor next to her. Reaching inside, she pulled out her tube of red lipstick. Then, resuming her pose, she puckered her lips, and applied the bright red color, just like the photo she'd seen of Marilyn Monroe on a poster board. She then leaned over, kissed the mirror, and stepped back, grinning at herself. "I've always wanted to do that." Turning, she grabbed her purse and sewing box off of the floor, then balanced them as she reached for her keys on the night stand.

She had played that entire morning away, as a result of the "release from mother-duties day" given to her by George and Ethel. They had taken the children to the home of George's dear friend in Kamas. It had been a mild winter, but there was still some snow up in the mountains, so George and his friend planned to hook the hay wagon up to the horses, and take the children for a ride up into the hills. Once there, they would roast hot dogs, and amuse themselves with outdoor adventures. George would definitely keep the young ones entertained and warm. Her children were in honorable, loving hands.

Claire's sense of humor, as well as her sincere concern for others' well being, were like a magnet for all those who attended the quilting class. Without Robert looking over her shoulder, she was very witty, breezy and even ingenious . That was one reason why she enjoyed the weekly quilting classes so much; she could just be herself. She also admired the way Sam taught the basic techniques, invariably recognizing the simple little achievements of her students, thus encouraging the process of piecing and designing with the fabric blends.

Since that first class, the women's progress had moved along smoothly, as Sam enlightened them with the basics of cutting and piecing, by using fundamental methods. They'd followed along with their pattern books, and had been further instructed by her drawings on the chalk board. She'd presented options, as well as new choices, using colors to generate the pattern designs with which each individual was working. Sam had always encouraged her students to let their imaginations flow; thus the unfamiliar had become the familiar.

Having no initial knowledge about the capabilities of her new students, Sam had paid close attention to their work, and been extremely thrilled with the choices they'd made, both of patterns, and fabrics, which they'd selected from a wide variety of colors available throughout the attractive, friendly quilt shop. The class was appropriately named "Block of the Month," since their goal had been to complete a new pattern, each month, from the chosen fabrics, all of which, when joined together, would become a full sized quilt, such as the one which now adorned Claire's four-poster.

Sam and Claire's friendship continued to blend just like the fabrics. They connected, not only through their creative sides, but also with their thoughts, sense of humor, faith, and love of family, just as delicate threads are collectively woven to make an artistic piece of cloth. The two of them were softly intertwined, with the love of the Savior being the thread that held them together. They could feel the angels blessing their friendship. They would soon find out that their companionship was like a gift they could unwrap each morning.

Many of their discussions would start, and end, with one confessing her weaknesses, while the other offered compassion, each incident tightening the bond between them. They would soon become inseparable, and unstoppable, as their life stories intertwined throughout the dreary, unforeseen days to come. They would partake daily from the Source of all illumination. They would believe in their dreams, cry in one another's arms, and have faith in each other as they lived their lives.

Sam and her family had moved to Woodland from Port Orchard, Washington, where her husband had worked as a tourist guide. Easily bored, he had a habit of jumping continually from one job to another, constantly looking for the yellow brick road, lined with gold. So, when his eye caught an ad in the local newspaper for a Woodland, Utah mink farm, his interest was naturally aroused. Not too many people would be a candidate for relocating and venturing out into unknown territory. Few, that is, other than Sam's husband Paul. It seemed he would never tire of moving Sam and their five children–two girls and three boys–from here to there, and back again. But his was always the final word, so, needless to say, they packed up their meager belongings, and headed out in their old Ford truck, packed like sardines in a can. Eighteen long miserable hours of travel to get to their destination, eating and bathing at the truck stops along the way.

It was a dreadful, humiliating trip, but as they pulled up to the old Campbell farm on Highway Forty-nine, just out of Woodland, Sam sighed in relief. There was a large, two story home, painted red, with cute white shutters on each window, and shaded by several green leafy trees. In the back stood a barn; no, a closer look revealed several barns of different sizes, with the sound of a gurgling creek coming from a place beyond the last little outbuilding. It was a comfy surrounding, and as they debarked from the truck, Sam spoke under her breath, "This could be home; *please Lord, let this be home."*

While her children ran in all directions, Sam stood behind Paul, and in a pleading tone asked,

"Paul, please let us make this our last stop; please let this be our home forever."

Paul studied his wife's anxious face. "This is the last stop, Sam; we'll make this work for sure."

A few hours later the lease and work agreement were signed, and Paul was in training to become a mink farmer, while Sam was on her way to a little grocery store in town called the Exchange Mercantile. As she turned the corner to go into the parking lot, her attention was grabbed by a quaint home across the street that looked like a fabric shop, and had a sign in the window, "Teacher Wanted." She continued to gawk in that direction until a sharp bump indicated that her tire had run over the curb, causing her to momentarily lose control of the wheel, and to nearly hit another car. She gasped, then smiled, as she hurriedly proceeded on in the same direction, finally locating a parking space by the back door of the Exchange.

She jumped down from the truck, banging the door twice before it latched, then ran across the street to apply for the teaching job. She knew she was well qualified. It didn't matter where Paul's dream took them, she was always able to find work teaching quilting classes: her respite from reality, as well as a means for putting food on the table.

She, of course, had been hired on the spot, and now here she was, several weeks later, with the class just winding down, and the group admiring each others' creativity with the fabrics they had chosen. Sam raised her voice so the chattering women would listen, "Ladies, please may I have your attention? I want you to be sure and circle your calendars on the dates of February twelfth through the fourteenth. I know this is Valentine's weekend, but you will really enjoy the quilting seminar that's been planned. I've been invited to be one of the instructors, but you need to book early, and reserve your rooms before January fifteenth. That only gives you a few days. I also know the Woodland's Valentine dance is scheduled on our return date. So plan ahead so we can all go to the dance with our husbands, or our dates. Okay, let's clean up, and I will see you next week."

Sam moved toward Claire, "You're going to the seminar, right?"

"I don't see why not. I'm sure that George and Ethel will watch the children for a day, and Robert will be flying in the next morning. I'll just need to find someone to watch them while we go to the dance, because I know that George wants to take Ethel. So I'll work on it."

"Maybe my oldest daughter could help tend. Ahhh, maybe not. She and Daniel are the same age, and I know she has a bit of a crush on him. He has called her several times to just talk, so we'd better scratch that idea."

Claire's mouth dropped open. "My son and your daughter? Where have I been?"

"I don't know, Girlfriend." Sam nudged her and smiled. "Where have you been?"

"Evidentially not in the right place. I wonder if he has said anything to George." Claire continued to gather up her rulers, scissors and fabrics, placing them in her sewing box. She grabbed her jacket, then gave Sam a hug. "I'll get my money to you before the dead line; we are rooming together, right?"

"I wouldn't have it any other way. And talk to George; I'm curious if Daniel has said anything."

Claire and George pulled into their driveways simultaneously. She got out of the car, opened the back seat door, and leaned in to get her portable sewing machine, which she carried to the back door of the house before setting it down. She then returned to get her sewing box, which she placed next to the machine.

Laughter drew her across the lawn to George's driveway, where she could hear his voice instructing the children on what to take out of the truck. When they saw Claire, they all started talking all at once.

"Wow," she chuckled, "one at a time, one at a time."

She could hear a grunt from George as he asked Daniel if he had hold of it. *Hold of what?* Claire wondered. The kids swarmed around her, jumping up and down, and pulling her to the back of the truck. "Look, Mom. George helped us build a bird house."

Claire's eyes broadened. This was not just a bird house; it was the most artistic birdhouse Claire had ever seen, the Taj Mahal of birdhouses. It was an eye-catching structure, with two or three smaller houses connected to the big one, and it was tall, almost as high as Claire, who now stood speechless. Well, George had done it again, exceeded all expectations with her children.

"Claire," he said, "we'll put this in the covered walkway, and brace it good 'til spring. Then we'll put it out in front of your kitchen window so you can hear the birds chirp in the mornings. Nothing like the sound of a sweet chirp to bring a smile to your day."

Ethel approached the group, carrying a basket. "We had a wonderful day, Claire. We hope you enjoyed your quilting class as well."

"Oh, very much so, Ethel. But, once again, I couldn't have done it without you and George filling in."

"My dear, we're the ones who are grateful, for grandchildren right next door. They keep us young. Now here are some left over ham slices and potato salad you and the children can finish up for dinner. I also think there are some fruit and cookies in there, as well."

While Claire and the children finished up the leftovers, cleaned up the kitchen, and bathed, she listened to each of them tell her what delighted them most about their day; it pretty much sounded like they simply loved everything best! Finally, the family gathered around Claire's bed for family prayer. Julie wanted to be voice, and Claire allowed her the privilege. She blessed Grandpa George and Grandma Ethel at least five times, then her brothers and sisters, the bird house, and Mommy, Amen. "Oops! And bless Daddy."

Claire lay in her bed, lonely for Robert, and sorry that he was missing so many little things that made his family lighthearted. She hugged the pillow tightly, and was just beginning to drift off, when she remembered that she hadn't asked George about Daniel and Heather. She would do that first thing in the morning.

CHAPTER 11

Robert's usual Friday night get-together with the guys from work, at the Last Stop Bar, had been cancelled, to allow them to attend the Denver Nugget's basketball game. Among his colleagues, the anticipation of the event had built all day, back and forth, from one office to the other, and Robert was relieved when, just before five o'clock, they all left, and he could get some work done. Since he'd been gone over the Christmas holidays, his working buddies hadn't known what his agenda would be upon his return, so they had only purchased tickets for themselves. That was fine with him; he needed to get some bids written up.

Robert had been back in Denver now for five weeks, working never-ending hours to get caught up from his absence over the holidays. Christmas with his family had been memorable: skiing with the boys, sleigh rides, snowmen, and "I love you"s being echoed from canyon walls, not to mention the butterfly kisses to save his heart. He savored the memory of intimate moments with Claire: holding her, protecting her, and loving her. He heaved a sigh; even George and Ethel had graciously thanked him for an experience never to be forgotten.

And yet, the minute he returned to his office, his heart began to hammer inside of him, anxiously anticipating the challenge of his work. So much was going on because of the growth of the company, much of which was a direct result of Robert's ingenious and pulsating ideas for product expansions, and price points. Oddly enough, many of his estimations had come as a consequence of his dad's early tutoring, which necessarily included his cut-throat mental attitude. Robert smiled ruefully over his growing awareness of who he was becoming. "I reckon the old man molded my life after all, because I'm turning out to be a reflection of him, one chilling decision after another."

Robert had talked to Claire the night before, and she had provided him with updates on all that was going on with the children. In a way, it wore Robert out, listening to her, so he worked on some accounts as he held the phone to his ear, saying *ah, hmm* and *really* in just the right places. His preoccupation came to a halt, however, when he heard her say, "But with your flight arriving Friday morning, you'll have the whole day and night with the children. You can pick them up at Ethel and George's by ten o'clock, and then I'll be home on Saturday, in time for the Valentine's Dance. The kids'll be so excited to have some "Dad" time, alone with you; how fun is that?"

"What? Just me and the kids? Where did you say you were going?"

"Robert, haven't you heard a word I've said?"

"Of course I have. I just want to make sure I have it right, so repeat the last part!"

Claire slowly repeated, word for word, their conversation, then added, "There is a couple going with us to the Valentine's dance; they just moved here from Washington. I can hardly wait for you to meet Sam and Paul; you'll enjoy associating with them. She's my best friend; we're soul sisters!"

"Hmm, soul sisters. That's somewhat intense, isn't it, Claire? Don't get too cozy with the husband till I meet him; I don't want him getting any ideas about you, you know, with me being gone and all."

"Robert! How dare you suggest such a thing! I would never even consider that kind of betrayal, and I'm offended by your presumption. How could you even assume I would have that intention?"

"Well, you never know, Claire; just be cautious, okay?" There were minutes of silence on the other end of the line, and Robert finally concluded with, "Love you, Hon. Give the kids a hug from Dad."

A cool, "Love you too," was repeated by Claire, before slamming the phone down.

Robert hadn't taken the time to call her back that morning. He'd arrived at the office early, and plunged into his work, where he'd remained bastioned for the day. He now gazed outside at the pitch blackness, aware that rain was gently hitting against his office window. Wow, where had the time gone? He glanced at his watch: ten fifteen. He had been working non-stop since five, when the guys had left for the game.

He was beat, and thinking a drink would relax him, he stretched his arms high above his head, then pushed himself back from the desk. His mind wandered for a few seconds, wondering if Shelly would still be working, and hoping she had the late shift. He liked the way she doted on him. Yup, that's what he needed: a drink and Shelly. Feeling cocky, he permitted his fanciful thoughts to take over his good judgment.

Robert slipped on his rain coat as he walked out the main door of the office building, nodding his head at the doorman. He then decided to walk to the Last Stop Bar instead of retrieving his car from the parking lot. It was only a few blocks, and he needed to stretch his legs. The rain was light, and felt good on his face. He didn't want to think; he just wanted to be detached, and guilt free, allowing the night to unfold, unfettered, before him. Each step he took echoed in a small splash on the pavement; each footstep brought him closer to Shelly.

The bar was overflowing with people, grouped together, celebrating the end of another work week. Robert studied the area for a place to sit, but every table was occupied, so he headed in the opposite direction toward the bar, found a stool at the end, and sat down, then stood again, removing his wet jacket, and placing it on the seat beside him.

Within minutes he could feel warm breathing on the back of his neck, and could smell the familiar perfume. Shelly leaned over his shoulder, and whispered in his ear, "I've missed you, Stranger. What would you like?"

Robert wanted to say, "You," but settled for a cold Coors. As she left his side, Robert took a deep breath. He liked what he felt: jitters, rapid heartbeat, arousal, and safe obscurity. He was alone; no one knew him here but the bar tender, and Shelly. He could be someone other than himself, unrestrained in his thoughts and behavior. Then, suddenly, he wondered, "Is this how my dad felt?"

The band was playing loudly, and the customers talking in high volume, the sizzling atmosphere increasing Robert's unsuppressed excitement. "One cold Coors for the gentleman at the bar." She stood at his side, placing the beer in front of him. He knew what this was leading to, and he continued to let it happen. Shelly whispered in his ear, "My car is in the repair shop. Could you give me a ride home? I get off at one."

Robert didn't even take the time to check his watch, but brought his lips close to her ear, and replied, "I walked to the bar from my office just a few blocks away. We can walk back together, and I'll give you a lift home."

It was done; he had executed what he'd thought would never happen. He'd crossed the line. Though he felt unscrupulous, he was pumped for the action ahead. In a split second, he had become the man he had loathed for all of his life.

Shelly Thompson had just turned twenty-six. She was originally from St. Louis Missouri, didn't know who her father was, and suffered a mother who was inebriated for most of each day. Shelly's grandma had cared for her until three years ago, when she passed away. Shelly knew, if she stayed in St. Louis, her mother would find out about the money Grandma had left her, so she packed what little she had into grandma's old brown suitcase, picked up the envelope that held seven thousand dollars, and walked away from the only safe place she'd ever known, heading for the bus station, several blocks away.

Numb to her state of affairs, she'd just continued buying tickets going west, until she ended up in Denver. She was totally alone, but had a fire in her belly that made her want to be somebody her grandma would be proud of. She found a little furnished apartment, and enrolled as a part-time student at the University of Denver, where she would pursue a degree in elementary education. Shelly wanted to give children the love and attention she'd never, herself, received. But she also needed to supplement her small inheritance, so searched the want ads of the local newspaper, where she noticed a job listing:

> Wanted – Waitress
>
> Evenings, 6:00 p.m. to 1:00 a.m.
>
> Experience not necessary
>
> Apply at The Last Stop Bar
>
> 2558 West Union Station Street
>
> (ask for Jim)

Shelly ripped the want-ad out of the paper, and headed for the bar. She met Jim, who was large in stature, his arms exhibiting muscles reminiscent of Popeye's. She could sense a certain tenderness in him, but she knew, in this business, he would be forced to squelch those tendencies, and remain tough. He flirted with her a bit, mesmerized by her large brown eyes, blond hair, and innocent face. She kept an eye on him as his gaze checked her out from head to toe; she knew all of her curves were in the right places, and occasionally her looks attracted the wrong kind of guys.

Jim nodded, and said in a deep rough voice, "Let me see your I.D. If that checks out, you're hired. She later learned that Jim's stern voice hid his mellow personality. He unvaryingly watched out for her, behaving like the father she never had.

The bar was now deserted, and Robert helped Shelly with her jacket, while Jim was hitting the light switches in the hall, one at a time, until the only light remaining was the Coors sign. It provided enough illumination for the police to see within the bar, as they performed their nightly rounds.

Robert and Shelly stepped with Jim out into the damp air, and waited for the older man to lock the huge wooden door behind them. "You two have a good night. See ya tomorrow, Shel." Jim shoved his hands into his brown leather jacket, and walked away, disappearing into the night. Robert and Shelly looked at each other as if they were surprised at being alone together.

Robert broke the silence, "I'm parked down the road a couple of blocks." Shelly innocently smiled at him, revealing a dimple in her right cheek which he had never before noticed. Man, she was young! He was at least ten years her senior, if not more.

She took hold of his arm, and they began strolling toward his car. After about twenty steps, she laid her head on his shoulder. When he abruptly stopped in his tracks, she raised her head, taken by surprise. Robert reached out both hands, cupping her face, and leaning in to kiss her lips, which were just as soft as he had expected. She put her arms slowly around his neck as the kiss continued.

Robert couldn't stop, didn't want to stop; he was on fire. Their hands traveled over each other's bodies, quickly and furiously, until Robert suddenly pulled back, out of breath. "My car is just about a block away," he rasped.

Her smile seemed innocent, but persuasive, as she grabbed his hand, and pulled him, running, to the parking lot, both of them giggling as if it were their first date, ever. The leather seats in the back of Robert's Cadillac were cold, but it didn't matter. And it didn't take long for Robert to realize that this encounter was far from a first date for Shelly. She was very experienced in love making, and he enjoyed every minute of it. Then, in the heat of the moment, he unwittingly whispered in her ear, "I love you, Claire!"

CHAPTER 12

Claire hung up the phone after calling Robert's number for over an hour; his work number had a recording, and there was no answer at his apartment. At 1:30 a.m. on a Sunday morning, where could he be? She knew he hadn't gone to the basketball game, because he told her earlier he had a lot of work to catch up on. She tried not to let her imagination run wild, but her nerves were getting the best of her. She was envisioning all sorts of things: a tragic mishap, or maybe he was really sick. Had he been in a car accident?

Claire arose from the side of the bed, and walked to the window. It was a clear, cold night, with a full moon dissipating the darkness. She shivered, and hugged herself with her arms, rubbing her hands up and down to take the chill out of her soul. Gazing at the moon, she whispered, "If you can see Robert, please keep him safe." She then returned to her previous position on the side of the bed, slipped under the covers, hugging the pillow next to her, and praying that her husband was okay.

Robert walked Shelly to her apartment door, and waited while she put the key into the lock, and heard the latch click. Then turning to face him, she asked, "Do you want to spend the night?"

Robert ran his hand through his hair to give himself a minute to think. "Yeah, I would, Sweetie, but I can't. I've still got some work to catch up on in the morning, so I can fly back to Utah on Friday."

Shelly didn't want to hear about his other life, and started kissing his neck, while her fingers ran through the back of his hair. Once again he began to tremble as they moved through the doorway, their locked lips expressing a continued desire for one another. The last things Robert was aware of were the full moonbeams dancing on the bed, and the breeze which blew in through the open window.

"Holy crap!" Robert sat bolt upright in bed, looking at his watch. "It's nine a clock." The sunbeams that were coming through the window, streaming across Shelly's bed, had awakened him from a deep, satisfied slumber.

Shelly covered her head with her pillow. "I want to sleep; pull the curtains shut, and hush up!"

"*Hush up?*" he repeated. "*Hush up?*" That was what his young daughter had told him at the cabin on Christmas Eve. He was going out the door to get the Christmas gifts and was making a racket in the main room, trying to find his boots. "Hush up, Daddy, or Santa will hear you!" And there stood five year old Julie, peeping out her bedroom door.

"Okay, Sweetie. Daddy was just getting a drink of water, but he will hush up so Santa can come." The event quickly played back through his mind, sickening him, as he realized how he had blown it. He'd thought he was invincible like his father, but did his father feel like a lowlife after he slept with another woman? How could he? He didn't have a little girl's voice ringing in his head, making him feel like a real jerk.

Robert dressed quickly and quietly, pain gnawing at the pit of his stomach as he tiptoed to Shelly's front door, and let himself out. Filled with self-loathing, he ran down the stairs and out into the sunshine to the curb, where his car was parked.

He was unlocking his apartment door when he heard the phone ringing, non-stop. Ringing, ringing, ringing. "I'm coming," he yelled, as he threw his keys onto the table by the front door.

"Hello," he said, with an irritated tone.

"Oh, my word, finally you're there. I've been worried sick all night! Are you all right? Where have you been? I've been crazy trying to find you, thinking something terrible had happened. Did something terrible happen?" Claire was sobbing in between each syllable.

"Uh, no. Nothing happened, Claire. Calm down. We had a . . . a . . . power outage. Yes, a power outage, and the phones weren't working, and I was just sitting here in the dark, with a flashlight, working on some paperwork, when I fell asleep. I'm sorry, Baby, for scaring you. I didn't think you would be calling me. The last time we talked, you were a little ticked with me over your new friends, so I was just buying time, so we could both calm down."

"I was, as you put it, ticked with you, but then I felt bad, and wanted to call and apologize. But then I couldn't get hold of you, and I panicked!"

"Well, I'm here now, Baby, and I'm glad you called." There was a pause. "It's real quiet there. Where're the kids?"

"It is quiet, isn't it? The boys are out in the garage with George, building derby cars for the scouting event in two weeks. George always likes to be ahead and prepared. Daniel is giving them a hand, and my friend's daughter Heather is here, helping with the painting."

"Claire, where is Julie?"

"She and Eliza are in their bedroom, playing with their Barbie dolls. Why do you ask?"

"Do you mind if I talk to Julie for a minute?"

"No, not at all. Just a second, and I'll get her."

"Hi, Daddy. When are you coming home? I rea-a-a-lly miss you."

"In just a few days, Punkin. I just wanted to know if you still have some butterfly kisses left?"

Robert could hear her giggle. "Yes, Daddy; I will save them for you. Do you have more tears to kiss away?"

"Yeah, Honey, I do."

CHAPTER 13

Claire loaded the last item into her suitcase, did a mental check, and then closed the bag. Sam would be here any minute to pick her up for the quilting seminar in Salt Lake City, at the Hilton Hotel. Ethel was wiping up the kitchen as Claire carried her cases to the front door. "I'll get George to help you carry them out," she said.

"Thanks, Ethel. My mind is going in a hundred different directions, so that would be helpful." Just then a car honked in the drive way, and George met Ethel at the door, just as she was going to call him.

"Can you help Claire to the car, Dear?"

"I was just coming to do that. Line the kids up, Ethel, so they can give her a Slurpee kiss, while I'm loading the suitcases and sewing machine." Ethel chuckled; she knew what he meant. They had made Slurpees earlier, the consumption of which had left each of the children with different colored Slurpee mustaches. All except Daniel; he was too old to be so silly.

"Well," Sam said, looking at Claire as she backed out of the driveway, "Salt Lake City, here we come!"

Claire waved goodbye to the children, whose faces were pressed against the living room window. "Wow," she said, "I'm really doing this: leaving my children for three days. I won't know how to act!"

Sam smiled. "We both won't know how to behave, but lets give it all we've got!"

It was a little after 10:30 the next morning when Robert knocked on the Watson's door. His plane had arrived about a half hour behind schedule, so he was a bit late picking up the kids. Nevertheless, he was prepared to be with his children, mentally and physically. He had called ahead and made reservations at Deer Creek Lodge in East Canyon, just over the hill from Woodland. He'd booked a master suite for the kids and himself, and another master suite for the caretakers of his children. He knew there would be some waiting while George and Ethel packed, but was in hopes that it would be a good surprise. It was a great time of year to go snowmobiling, and they would be home early Saturday.

The door opened, and there stood Ethel with her warm smile. "Well," Robert said, "how flexible are you?"

She gave him a questioning look. "What are you up to this time, Robert?" He laid out for her a summary of his agenda, and she let out a whoop and a holler. Everyone came running, and Ethel told them they had been taken by surprise once again. No one in the group was questioning the time frame, but since they had to pull it all together so quickly, they scattered in every direction. Robert laughed delightedly. He didn't know which way to go, or who to help, so he waited outside to load the luggage into the rental van.

They arrived in time to have lunch at the Lodge, then the men and boys went to check in for the snowmobiles. Daniel was given one of his own; George teamed up with Davis, and Robert climbed on with Joey.

Ethel and the girls were nervous about riding the machines, so chose to do their sightseeing on the horse drawn sleigh; they had liked it before, so they knew it was a safe choice. Hours later, they all met in the lodge to share their stories, as they gathered for a dinner buffet. After the meal, George and Ethel elected to take the boys with them to their sleeping quarters, and Robert smiled at his two girls saying, "Okay, my little princesses, let's go get your bubble bath ready."

After their bath, Eliza, ten, and Julie, five, put on their pajamas, said their prayers with Daddy, and gave him kisses as he tucked them into bed. They were asleep within minutes, exhausted from the merriment of the day, and Robert sat in the chair across the room, reflectively watching their innocent slumber.

He was such a jerk. This whole adventure had been planned because of the deep guilt he was experiencing over the episode with Shelly. This, right here, was who he was: a husband, a father; a lover, yes, but only with his wife. That is what they had vowed. "Man," he said to himself, "I've really messed up." He hung his head down, and was looking at the floor, when he felt a small soft hand on his cheek. Lifting his chin, he saw Julie standing at his side. "Daddy, I forgot to give you your butterfly kisses!"

CHAPTER 14

"What color are we painting your toenails?" Sam's curiosity was getting the best of her, since Claire hadn't been able to decide on the color for her fingernails, and consequently had painted each one a different hue. They were red, blue, hot pink, yellow, and her little pinky was purple! The two of them were sitting on the plush carpet in their hotel room, wearing their brand new Betty Boop pajamas. Earlier, during their lunch break, as they'd strolled down the city block, they were drawn to a women's specialty shop, where, once inside, they were immediately attracted to the rack containing sleep wear. They took a quick glance at each other, then began searching for their sizes, as if they were in a marathon.

After the purchase they knew they were short on time, so they grabbed a couple of hot dogs from a street vender, and then ran as fast as they could back to the hotel where the classes were being held. Scurrying down the hall, they slid into door number two, knocking down the sign which advertized: PAPER PIECING BY RUBY BAKER. Every lady in the room turned her head toward them to see what all the racket was about, while the teacher, being very professional, continued to call roll.

"Sam Barnes."

Sam took a deep breath, walked gracefully to her seat, and politely responded, "Here."

"Claire Jensen."

Claire was still gasping for air. She'd stuffed the rest of her hot dog into her mouth just as she and Sam had hit the sign. She quickly choked down what remained, and was left gagging as she tried to say, "Here."

"Well," the teacher said, "this is going to be an interesting class. Welcome, Claire!"

It had been a rewarding afternoon, but perhaps not as soul satisfying as the evening that followed. The hour was now getting late; however, as Claire and Sam climbed onto their big king-sized bed, and sat facing each other, Indian style, they continued to tell the stories of their lives, recounting their journeys. As one would relate an incident, and the other share a tale, it was difficult to believe all that had occurred over the relatively short span of their lives.

They discussed the uncomfortable details about their pregnancies and deliveries. Sam had a smaller frame than Claire, and carried her babies high, so labor was very drawn out. In fact, the doctors wanted to do a C-section to deliver Heather, but Sam refused, choosing to have her naturally. She prayed for divine help, and within an hour Heather was born.

Claire's deliveries, on the other hand, were not difficult, in spite of the fact that Daniel had weighed nine pounds. "The problem wasn't the weight," Claire explained, scooting next to Sam, and putting her arm around her. "The problem was that the doctor asked if some interns could watch the delivery. I'm thinking one, maybe two. Oh, no! The door opened, and the whole room filled with young men, training to be doctors, and I'm the lesson. Nothing like exposing yourself to the world!

"So how did you meet your knight in shining armor, Sam?"

"Oh, it was very romantic," she giggled. "He was working at McDonalds, in Portland, after he graduated from high school. That was my home town too. Anyway, I went in with my two girlfriends, and this boy who took our order just kept looking at me, and making me blush. We all just ordered hamburgers, and that's what my two friends got. But mine showed up with fries. I told him I didn't order fries, and he said, 'It's on the house.' Well, I didn't dare tell him I hated fries, so I ate them anyway, and was sick all night long. I didn't go back for about a week, even though I kinda thought he was cute. When I did go back, I ordered a hamburger, and, please, no fries. The order come out, and guess what? Fries! I should have guessed, right then, that if I married him, he was never going to listen. He asked me out, and convinced me that our lives together would be nothing short of a bed of roses. Well, so far it's just been a hard old inner spring mattress!" Claire, by this time, was laughing her head off. "Now, your turn, Claire. How did you meet Robert?"

"I don't know if I should tell you; it's so very much like a fairy tale."

Sam popped some chocolate into her mouth. "Okay, I'm ready to swoon."

"Well, it was graduation night and we–you know, friends and classmates–were up on Memorial Hill, celebrating, and he cruised in with some of his friends, and was driving this unbelievable red Impala convertible. He motioned for me to come dance with him, and when I

59

saw those dreamy blue eyes, and his cute dimpled smile–what can I say? He had me with his first, 'Hello.' Okay, Sam, so what's your deepest, darkest secret?"

Sam's eyes fell, and she plucked absently at the hem of her pajamas. "My deepest, darkest secret would be that I have fallen out of love with my husband. He has been such a con man; he's always full of promises, so sure that he's just about to find the pot of gold. We go from one destination to another, always following his dream, but never finding the rainbow. I'm tired of being poor, I'm sad for my children, and I pray my boys will not walk in their father's footsteps.

"He's harsh, and to the point with everything he says to them, to the degree of being intimidating, so I'm very protective of them when he's home. But, I must say, since we arrived in Woodland, he's mellowed out a bit. I just hope he sticks to this job longer than all the ones he's tried before."

"Wow, Sam, that's deep. In a way I'm in the same position. I don't mean that I'm falling out of love with Robert, but I have a lot of fears lately about where our marriage is headed. Robert makes a lot of money, and that's what he uses to make up for his neglect. He just doesn't want to be a 'stick-around-at-home' dad. He's great at sweeping you off your feet with creative adventures, but you would never see him stay around the house too long. The children and I are too overwhelming for him, day in and day out. Besides, he's scared he'll miss out on something in the big business world. I'm afraid he's becoming more and more like his father: a playboy. His mother didn't have the vigor to leave her husband or his money, and if Robert ever cheated on me, I'd be just like her, hanging in there for the security. Heaven forbid that he even goes that way, but how would I be able to provide for my family without him?"

"Hmm." Sam reached for another chocolate. "Okay, this is getting gloomy; let's change the subject, and fast, before we have a meltdown."

"Do you want to know my deepest secret?" Claire sniffed, and wiped her nose with the back of her Betty Boop pajama cuff. Sam nodded her head, holding out a Kleenex box. Both of them blew their noses, ready then to continue their pillow talk. Claire, still trying to bury the sounds of her weeping, said, "Well, after my last child, I had a tummy tuck."

"What! No way. Let me see." Sam kneeled in front of Claire so she could have a better look. "Wow! You really did. I would have never guessed that one." Sam puffed up her pillow, and leaned back against it. "Okay, my turn. My greatest desire is to fulfill a promise I have made to myself." She sighed, and continued, "Before I die, I want to make sure all five of my children have a pieced quilt, made by me, so I can cover them with my love as they sleep."

"Sam," Claire whimpered, "what a touching ambition. I'm sure you'll able to achieve that goal; after all, you have a lifetime to do it in." She reached over and hugged Sam.

"Okay," Sam giggled, "now let's draw a wild card for our topsy-turvy minds. What would we do with Elvis, if we had him alone for an hour?"

Claire grinned. "Hmm, a whole hour. Hmm, give me a minute, Sam, this is a hard one. I know, I know. I would lie in a hammock, and have him stand over me gently pushing me back and forth while he sang, 'I can't help falling in love with you.' What about you? What would you do?"

"I would sit out on a beach somewhere, and have him hold my hand, while he sang as many songs as he could to me, ending with 'I want you, I need you, and I love you.'"

"Neither one of us added a kiss; I wonder if he's a good kisser."

"We'll never know," said Sam. "I don't think we are on his to-do list."

Hours dwindled away as the two friends continued with a debate about the best movies, and best actors, and whether they could go a day without a cold Coke. Sam said she could; Claire said she didn't even want to try. When considering what frightened them the most about growing old, they agreed that it was not learning to forgive, before it was too late.

"We've shared some beautiful thoughts, Sam. Wow, it makes me want to start crying again. Come here, Girlfriend, and let's seal this night with a hug. Friends forever and ever." The two sets of Betty Boop pajamas melded together, as souls bonded through this precious night of sharing that would never be forgotten, forming a friendship that was fortified by their faith in each other, their warm hearts, and never-ending prayers.

The quilting class that Sam had been invited to instruct went way beyond the ladies' expectations. She taught the ins and outs of maintaining your sewing machine, demonstrated different machine stitches, and then walked around to each student, showing them the techniques they could apply at home on their own machines. She also did a demonstration on binding, both by hand, and with a machine. At the end of the class she gave hints and helps for pressing strip sets, and borders, and putting them all together.

During their break, all of Sam's class went into the hotel's cafeteria, where they were offered a choice of fruits, drinks, and pastries, including a large assortment of doughnuts. The other ladies filled their plates with a variety of the items, but Claire's mind was on how much she had eaten on this retreat, and whether she'd be able to get into her red dress for the dance. Therefore, she just chose fruits. Sam looked at her plate, and giggled, "Can't believe you didn't get one of those yummy chocolate doughnuts, Claire."

"I know. I'm worried I won't fit into my dress when I get home." Claire watched as all of the ladies at her table enjoyed their pastries, not to mention the nice chocolate doughnuts, while she virtuously ate her fruit. Her resolve was beginning to weaken, when the lady sitting next to her mentioned that all those yummy chocolate doughnuts were gone. "Oh, great, Sam. I'll always wish that I'd had one." Then, glancing at a table close by, she noticed a gentleman was standing to leave, his big untouched chocolate doughnut about to be abandoned!

She nudged Sam, whose mouth dropped open. "You wouldn't!"

"Well, he left it, and it hasn't been touched. What the heck!" She bravely stood, and walked nonchalantly toward the table which held the coveted delicacy. Causally dipping sideways, she swiped up the doughnut, and returned to the table of grinning women.

Sam said, "Way to go, Girlfriend. That was brave. But, like you said, he left it." Just then the man reappeared with a fresh glass of milk, stopped dead in his tracks, and stood staring at his empty plate. He didn't notice that everyone at the other table was covering her mouth with her hands, trying to hold back laughter, as Sam and Claire ducked out at the opposite side of the room. Once in the foyer, they bent over laughing, gasping for air. "Well," said Sam, "this is one I will never forget."

Claire wiped the tears from her eyes, "I know, Girlfriend. We'll take this one to our graves!"

Sam and Claire were struggling to get everything re-packed into the trunk. For some reason they were leaving with more than they had brought. Of course, the most valued of their newly acquired possessions needed no suitcase: quirky, crazy, treasured memories that would last them a lifetime. It felt good to have a friend like Sam; at this point Claire couldn't imagine life without her. They were two peas in a pod, blood sisters (or chocolate sisters), friends forever and ever. But the frolic was over; it was time to head back to Woodland, to be mothers, and wives–and girlfriends.

CHAPTER 15

Claire juggled her suitcase and shopping sacks as she turned the knob, then used her foot to push the door open, expecting shouts of delight, and a warm welcome upon her return home. But there was nothing; the house was silent. She set the suitcase down just inside the door, and headed to the bedroom to deposit the other bags onto her bed. Where was everyone? Then she heard a car or truck pull into the driveway, and within minutes there were the shouts she'd been missing.

Almost immediately the gang was coming through the back door, not knowing that Mom was home, but delighted to see her suitcase leaning against the wall. Robert traveled a few steps behind the children, noticing the case, and uttering a sigh of relief that he had made it home just in time.

Claire came out of her bedroom with hands resting on her hips. "And where have my little Munchkins been?"

"With their dad, killing time till Mom came home," Robert voice muttered. He then stepped out from behind Daniel, smiling broadly, and revealing the dimples that Claire adored. He took her in his arms, saying, "I get to kiss Mommy first." The kiss was tender, but the children still groaned from embarrassment, except for Daniel; he timidly watched to see how it was done.

"Okay," Claire announced, "let's all go to the living room, and you can tell me where your dad took you against your will, snatching and forcing you to go dally the day away. Then you can open the gifts I brought home for you."

Eliza laughed, "You're funny, Mom. But, come to think about it, we were screaming."

"Yeah," Joey joined in, "screaming 'cause we were going somewhere fun."

Robert was on the couch, and motioned for Claire to come sit beside him. He then held her close in his arms while they listened to the children's version of the snowmobiling adventure at the lodge. "Thank heavens George and Ethel went with them," Claire thought. It sounded kind of fast and furious for just one night. Eventually the excitement wore down, and the kids went off to play with their new gifts from Mom.

Robert nibbled on Claire's neck, and whispered in her ear, "What did you get for your hubby?"

"Some wonderful cologne. The salesman said *Santos* is all the rave for men. Hold that thought, and I will be right back." Claire scooted to the bedroom, and quickly returned to sit on Roberts lap. "Here, my dear husband, let me put just a drop on your neck, and I will tell you if the salesman was right." The fragrance was enticing, and she smiled. "The salesman was right. "Now, my dear hubby, let's go get ready for the dance, before we forget we have a house full of innocent children."

Robert talked above the roar of the shower, "Who's tending the kids tonight?"

"Oh, I completely forgot to tell you. Miss Peggy volunteered the other night at our sewing class; she will be over by seven thirty."

"This will be an interesting night for them. Do they know?"

"They will in a minute."

Claire heaved a sigh as Robert zipped up her silky red dress; she actually had breathing room, so didn't regret the chocolate doughnut after all. She smiled at herself as she turned sideways to check her hair and makeup. In the mirror she noticed Robert grinning at her with a smirk on his face.

"What are you smiling about, Mr. Robert Jensen?"

"I'm smiling because I keep falling in love with you more, minute by minute, hour by hour, lifetime to eternity. And why are you smiling at yourself in the mirror?"

"Oh, I just had a flashback of a doughnut. It's a girl thing, but it made me smile, anyway. I'm also smiling because I'm so happy when you're home, Robert. It's words like you just said to me that I hang onto when I go to sleep at night, in an empty bed."

"Yes, M' Lady, but just remember it's that job that I fly out to that allows you to play, and shop, and look so marvelous. Geez, Claire!" Robert stood and stepped behind her, wrapping his arms around her waist. "I want you to always remember how basic our love is for each other, and always think of this moment, and the deep affection we have, one for another. I will never stop loving you and the kids, no matter what."

Claire swiftly turned to face him. "I know you love us, Robert, but you're acting like you're going to die or something. Stop! You're scaring me."

"I don't mean to scare you; I just don't want you to ever forget this moment, here and now, and what we are feeling."

Just then the door bell chimed, interrupting Claire's thoughts. Tenderly she asked, "Are we okay, Robert? You and I, are we all right?"

He leaned over and kissed her cheek, using his thumb to wipe away her tear, very gently, so he wouldn't smear her makeup. "Yes, Honey, we're good."

"Who's tending us?" Daniel said in protest. "I thought you said Heather and I could tend!"

"I did say that, Daniel, and you can. You'll just have Miss Peggy here for extra help."

"Ahh, Mom–" his words were cut off, as he watched his dad help Miss Peggy through the door; he was carrying all of the games, and ice cream she had brought. She even had Heather with her; maybe this was going to be a cool night after all. Daniel smiled at Heather. "Here, Dad, I'll help Miss Peggy."

Claire and Robert walked toward the stone building called the Amusement Hall; it had been built in 1889 and was one of the historic landmarks in Woodland. Robert held Claire's hand as they took the two steps up to the wide wooden door. They were to meet Sam and Paul in the foyer, and while they waited, Robert took his jacket and Claire's wrap to the coat check-in area on the far right of the entrance. Upon his return he stood gallantly next to Claire, where everyone who came in stopped to chat, making them feel like the assigned Valentine's greeters.

Then Sam walked in with Paul close behind her. She looked so elegant in her white silk full-length dress, accented with mink cuffs and collar. She was beautiful! Paul looked very handsome also, but Claire couldn't believe how stunning Sam was. Not that she hadn't already known she was a beautiful woman, but there was a reverent glow surrounding her tonight, and Claire was awed by it.

Paul was not a tall man; in his cowboy boots, he stood only a little above Sam's height. He was clean shaven, except for a little mustache on his upper lip, and his eyes were a deep brown that matched his hair color. His shoulders were broad, and Claire thought he could have just walked out of a western movie. Yeah, that was it; he looked like a shorter John Wayne. "Not bad," Claire said to herself, "not bad at all."

The couples moved into the dance hall, and surveyed their surroundings. The floor was actually built with spring wires underneath the boards, so as you danced, it added a little bounce to your steps. The seniors, including George and Ethel, had decorated the hall with glittery red hearts, all types of flower bouquets, large cardboard cutouts of cupids, as well as vintage boys and girls, giving each other Valentines. The whole theme was extremely clever, delightful and very romantic. You could hear the "oohs," and "ahs" over the decorations, as everyone mingled. Meanwhile, Claire and Robert circled the room with Sam and Paul in tow, introducing them to all the folks from town.

The Watsons approached, and George asked if he could have the first dance with Claire. Robert took hold of Ethel's hand, and replied, "Only if I can have the first dance with the second love of my life."

Ethel smiled. "My, my, Robert, you do have a way with women; you melt their hearts, and then sweep them off their feet."

The master of ceremonies put on a waltz, and the couples held one another as they lightly danced around the ballroom. It wasn't long before they were twisting to the Chubby Checkers all- time hit, following which the men lined up on one side and the women on the other so they could do the stroll. Then, of all things, George encouraged the emcee to play the bunny hop. By the time it was over, everyone was ready for refreshments.

As they sat around a table adorned with Cupids, the foursome thoroughly enjoyed one another's company. Soon Paul leaned toward Robert, asking, "Do you mind if I have a dance with your lovely wife?"

"Not at all, Paul. And that opens the door for me to dance with your beautiful wife."

Paul was a very smooth dancer, but Claire wasn't comfortable with his firm hand on her back, trying to pull her closer with each twirl. Finally, she smiled at him, saying, "My husband is a very jealous man, so I would appreciate it if we danced at arms' length."

"Whatever the lovely lady wants," he replied.

Clair continued talking about Sam, and the way she so willingly shared all of her many talents with others. "Yes," said Paul, "she is the love of my life, and the pillar of our family."

The emcee, at that point, approached the microphone, and announced the last song of the night: *When I Fall In Love*, by Nat King Cole. As the music played, Robert said the words softly into Claire's ears, promising her his complete heart, and undying love. The Valentine dance had been all that Claire could hope for, and more. Robert was such a romantic, and when the music come to an end, their lips met, dreamily completing a beautiful night.

CHAPTER 16

It had been three rainy, cold weeks in Denver since Robert had come back from Utah. KARS, the company that employed him, was getting ready to stimulate the Nevada area by providing them with a giant warehouse, full of parts for all car makes. There was a lot of work to do before the Las Vegas opening, and he needed to be accurate with the ordering. Feeling tired and out of sorts, he noted that the wet weather appropriately matched his gloomy mood. He had been pounding away, day and night, on this Vegas project. "Suck it up, man; this is why you get paid the big bucks," he said to himself. "Keep going till you finish this count, then cut it off for the night."

He continued to work for another hour before closing the huge ordering books, and straightening his desk top. He arose, bent over to stretch out his legs, and walked to the huge window that overlooked the city. The lights that glistened in a few selected windows of other buildings disclosed the fact that he was not the only one who was working late. His reflection in the dark glass, superimposed over the city beyond, struck him with a fleeting awareness of his own insignificance, when compared to the world; yet he knew he had the capability of affecting many lives as he lived his own.

He sighed, then took a couple of steps to the coffee pot sitting on the warmer. Robert picked up his customary mug, the one that Joey and Julie had given him last Christmas. He reflected back instantly, remembering the looks on their faces as they waited for him to open their gift. He'd told them it was a present he could use daily, and he had actually kept that promise. He slowly sipped his coffee, his free hand slipping into his pocket, and nervously playing with the change inside, as his thoughts raked over his life. Where was it headed, and did he really want it go in any other direction?

Robert enjoyed being home, but after a few days he never failed to get antsy. He took delight in being the hero to his household, impressing them with gifts, and trips, and memories, but when it came down to the children's basic needs, he was a lost cause. The boys were involved in numerous activities, in the midst of which the girls needed to be car-pooled to their tap dance classes. And, even though their piano lessons were provided by Ethel, next door, the house got chaotic with everyone going in all directions. Robert's nerves unfailingly got the best of him; he liked everything quiet, calm, and productive, like his work environment. Whenever Claire started filling him in on everything, and everybody, it became nerve-wracking.

Robert knew he was inadequate compared to George, who had become a safe haven to his children. Actually Robert was very relieved that his neighbor had taken over, since he, himself, didn't have the patience nor the time, what with flying in and out so much. Hell, maybe he should put George on his payroll, to make up for all he did, day in and day out, trying to erase the neglect imposed by an absent, self-absorbed father.

Robert relished his role as Superman to Claire, sweeping her off of her feet with romance, smothering her with his love and desire, promising all that she wished for during each of his stays. Nevertheless, he knew that he could no longer make those promises, not anymore, because Shelly was always in the back of his mind. Occasionally he would panic over the guilty realization that he should be with Claire all the time, but then he'd get the jitters, wanting to move on, to get back to work where he had more control, and where he could be closer to Shelly. He knew he was in helter-skelter mode, but for the time being, he decided to stay that way, and see how long he could play the game.

After all, he had been sort of a hero on the night of the Valentine Dance. When he'd escorted Claire to the car, he'd held her arm gently, opening the door, and helping her in. Then he'd come around to the other side, opened his door and slid in beside her, immediately starting the car, and mentioning to Claire that it would take a few minutes to warm. As they'd waited, Robert had pulled out a little gold box from the glove compartment, smiling that dimpled grin that made Claire's eyes glisten, and handed the box to her. She'd slowly untied the ribbon, and pulled the lid off, gasping at the beautiful gold pendent, bearing a gold heart, and showcasing a diamond in the center. Words were not necessary, as Claire's teary-eyed look explained exactly how she felt. At that moment, Claire had known that Robert adored her, as he'd gently clasped the gift around her neck.

Now, sitting at his desk, he was gazing at another gold pendant, identical to the one he'd given Claire. It had been tucked away in his office drawer ever since his return from Utah. For the last three weeks, he had purposely been avoiding The Last Stop Bar. And, each Monday morning, the guys at work would mention that Shelly had asked about him when they'd gone for drinks on the preceding Friday.

Robert was not only busy with the new distribution center; he was working on his cowardly backbone. He was pumping up his courage to tell Shelly how sorry he was for uttering Claire's name as they were making love. He had hopes that the gift would enhance his apology, and get him back into her good graces. He liked her youth, her energy, and the way she made love. He felt many fresh emotions when he was with her, and he enjoyed the vitality she brought back into his life. He needed a mistress.

Bingo! Now he knew why his Dad cheated.

Robert took the option, once again, to walk to the Last Stop in the drizzling rain. Pulling the collar up on his slicker, and placing his hat at an angle to keep the moisture from his face, he took a deep breath, and expelled the air from his lungs. He had been cooped up for hours, and needed to revive his thinking, and clear his mind of paper work.

As Robert stepped into the bar, he quickly took off the wet hat and coat, placing them on the rack down the hall by the restrooms. With a couple of strides he entered the mens' room, and took a gander at himself in the mirror, making sure he didn't look as frazzled as he felt. His reflection verified that he was unruffled, and better looking than he had any right to be. "Not bad," he said to himself, "for a man who will hit the big forty next year."

Robert's agenda tonight was to proceed to the next chapter of his life. He would never let his choices get to the point that he destroyed people, like his dad had destroyed his mother. But he reasoned that, if he ventured out slowly, he could have two loves, without hurting either of them. He just needed to know what Shelly wanted: future companionship, or just a one night stand. What if she wasn't really interested in him? She could possibly have a boyfriend, and had just slept with him due to the passion of the moment. Was it too soon to ask? Then Robert took another deep inventory of himself. If he pursued his own selfish desires, how could he not destroy Claire? He would have to be very careful to cover his tracks. The children would be fine; regarding them, George filled Robert's shoes comfortably.

He made himself crazy at times, the way his thoughts bounced back and forth, wishy washy, but at the present moment he was gung-ho for an affair. Then his nerves, or maybe his conscience, sent a message to the pit of his belly, questioning his moral standards. He just needed a drink to calm down; then he would take the next step.

As he claimed a stool at the end of the bar, Jim's husky voice asked, "The usual, Robert?"

"Yeah, the usual," said Robert, as he turned to search the room for Shelly.

"She's not here."

Robert spun back around to look at Jim dubiously, his voice exhibiting panic as he sternly asked, "You mean she's moved?"

"No, man. Take it easy. She called in sick tonight. I think it's just a touch of the flu."

Robert thought to himself, "The flu, or some other guy?"

"Give her a call; it will probably make her feel better. She's been moaning for weeks 'cause you ain't been in."

"She has?"

"Yeah, she has. And I'm tellin' ya, mister, don't play games with my princess, or I'll have to hurt you. She's fragile, being out on her own, and all. You're the first guy she's been with since she moved to this town. So I'm watching every step ya take, da ya understand me?"

Robert would have to be an idiot not to understand Jim's words, especially with the guy's face just inches away from his own. Robert gulped his beer down, and thumped the mug back onto the bar with force. Jim stood firm, keeping an eye on him, and not even blinking at the sound of the mug hitting against the surface.

"She's safe with me, Jim. I'll protect her. You got my word."

Jim stretched out his hand. "Let's shake on it, partner."

Robert grasped the offered hand. Jim's grip was stronger than his own, yet they both knew the understanding between them was solid. Robert stood, and walked to where his coat and hat were hanging. Retrieving them from the hooks, he noted that they were relatively dry now. He waved his hand at Jim as he stepped out of the bar.

Even though the rain had ceased, there was a chill in the night air, and Robert shivered as he walked back to the office to collect his car. Once inside, he let the motor idle for a few minutes, and as he left the parking lot, he could feel the heater warming his body.

He didn't know if Shelly would even be awake; if she didn't feel well, she may have crawled into bed early. It was almost one in the morning, but as he turned the corner to her apartment, he could see her lights were still on. He took an inventory of the area, but couldn't see any other cars parked out front. Even though Jim had assured him that she wasn't seeing anyone else,

Robert didn't want to walk in on an uncomfortable situation. He wished to continue seeing Shelly, but he shied away from physical confrontation, even when he was challenged.

He tapped on her door, and in a low tone said, "Shelly, it's Robert." He could hear her soft steps coming toward the door, and the subsequent clicks as she released the locks. The door slowly opened, and Robert gazed upon her teary-eyed face. Before he was even inside, he held his arms out to her, and she jumped into them, wrapping her legs around his waist, and burying her head in the hollow of his neck, the power in her grip evenly matching his own.

Robert's words were soft in her ear, "Don't cry, Sweetie; I'll never leave you again." As she lifted her head and kissed him gently, he could taste her salty tears. With Shelly's body still clinging to him, he walked through the door, shutting it with his foot, and carried her to the sofa, never interrupting the kiss. There he gently continued to hold her, until their passion ignited; then he carried her into the bedroom.

The sun filtered through Shelly's window, releasing a new day. Robert had held her throughout the night, and now, as her head lay on his shoulder, he watched her sleep, moving his fingers back and forth along her arm. She stirred, then opened her deep brown eyes, and looked up at him.

"Good morning, Baby." She smiled, and nestled closer to him, if that were possible. Then Robert whispered in her ear, "I love you."

She stirred within the circle of his arm, and whispered back, "I love you too, but it scares me."

"Don't be scared, Shelly. I'll always take care of you. I'll be here for you."

"But what about your family?"

Robert didn't move. "Who told you about my family?"

"When you didn't come back for weeks, I asked Steve, and he told me about your family in Utah"

"I'm sorry you had to hear it from him, Shelly. I was going to tell you, but I wasn't sure what we have, or what we want, or if I should even flirt with the thoughts of us being together. It's going to be complicated, Shelly, but I want you to know I care for you a great deal. I'm torn; I love my family, but when I'm with them, I'm thinking about you. It's driving me crazy."

She moved from his hold, posing in front of him. "Robert, I love you. I know that sounds crazy, when we've only known each other for such a short time, but I do. My life is unbearably empty when you're not here. I won't put pressure on you concerning your family, but please let

71

me be charmed by you when you're here. Let's throw our morality to the wind, and let ourselves fall deeper in love. There's no rhyme nor reason for my existence without you."

He circled his arms around her, kissing her passionately, non-stop, while his heart was breaking for what he was doing, but not wanting to vary this moment. When he finally released her, he whispered, "I can only promise you a day at a time, Baby."

"I'll take it," she whispered back.

Hours later Robert and Shelly showered, dressed and headed out for a day of romance. They were like two teens, full of energy, anxious to more fully explore each other's inner beings, to discover their likes and dislikes. It was a lighthearted day, full of unforgettable memories, from shopping, and viewing the landscape from the ski lifts, to roasting hot dogs in a fire pit, abandoned due to the winter season. Robert and Shelly found it exhilarating to build the fire and hover around it for their lunch. As the daylight ran into the dusk, Robert took Shelly shopping for clothes, and let her buy her heart out, but suggested she choose a special dress for tonight. She looked at him quizzically.

"Relax, my dear, your knight in shining armor is taking you to the Winter Ball"

Shelly's mouth dropped open. "How did you get tickets for the ball?"

"I never reveal my sources, dear one, but I do have a little pull in this city." He relished the expression on her face, and the brightness of her eyes. He loved pampering her, and looked forward to the days that lay ahead, getting to know her better, and accepting whatever it was that drew them together.

Shelly looked lustrous on his arm as they walked into the ball at the Union Station. No one there knew who they were, but as they danced, Robert heard many affirmative comments, mostly about how extremely beautiful Shelly was, and how she was the image of Cinderella. He also heard, and chose to ignore, a few remarks about their age difference.

As they danced, Robert's hand went into his pocket, pulling out the pendant with the diamond. He gently placed it upon her throat, kissing her, as his hands moved to the back of her neck, where he clasped together the ends of the chain. Shelly felt like a little girl in one of the fairy tales she used to make up; but this one was unquestionably real.

CHAPTER 17

The sun was shining as Robert drove his new red Mustang GT V8 convertible off the car lot. Sun loving people like himself snapped up thousands of these Mustangs, as soon as they hit the dealerships. Needless to say, Robert was one of the first in line, as soon as he'd been informed that this would be the reward from his boss for all of his ingenuous ideas regarding the distribution centers. His concepts were helping them thrive and grow, expanding into more states. Robert was a happy-go-lucky man.

He felt youthful and virile, full of vitality. His weekend with Shelly had been a daydream come true. Then, on Sunday night, his boss had called him, proposing that Robert go to San Diego, check on the warehouse there, and then continue on to Las Vegas for at least two weeks to get the plant ready for its grand opening on April First. The tab would be picked up by the company, naturally.

Robert squealed into the company's parking lot, attracting attention from several bystanders, who stepped back to avoid being run over. He smoothly pulled into his reserved spot, proudly flaunting the new toy to his co-workers, who were also parking their cars. He had a skip in his walk, with his jacket flipped over one shoulder, held by his left hand, while his right hand grasped his briefcase. Heads turned as he moved toward his office.

Steve, seated at his desk, watched him pass, then jumped up and followed close behind. "What's up, Robert? You look like the cat that ate the mouse."

"I did! We all did. This company is on a roll, thanks to all of you. Under my leadership," he smugly added. "I'll be printing out new assignments today, as per Mr. Bethers' instructions."

Randy Bethers had been a good friend to Robert when they attended high school, and Robert had been pleased when his old buddy had opened the door for him to expand the company Randy had inherited upon his father's death. The day Randy called him at the station in Woodland was the best day of his life. "Hmm, back up," his mind protested. What about marrying Claire and having the children? "Okay, okay, the seventh happiest day of my life," he murmured to himself.

All lights were green for Robert to go on a month's long business trip; he just had to make a couple of phone calls, then he was out of there to catch his plane. After shutting the glass door to his office, for privacy, he dialed his home number. "Claire, this is Hubby. How ya doin?" Oh, man, he shouldn't have asked. She immediately went into one of those detailed, melt down news reports of all that had happened in the last three, going on four, weeks. He didn't think she was even breathing between her words.

"Honey . . . Honey . . . Claire! Stop just a second. Listen to me, Baby. I've got to catch a flight in a couple of hours, so I wanted to share some good news on my end. The company has had a great financial year, and all systems are go to get the warehouse in Vegas opened by April. Regretfully, I can't help the boys with their little league baseball this time, like I did last year. Claire, I know . . . I know . . . but this is the way we live, Hon; it's our lifestyle. I'm flying out to the coast, and then on to Vegas. I know this sounds like a drawn-out time away from home, but I have no choice. Hon, I won't be flying in to Utah till after the grand opening.

"Claire, don't go emotional on me. Try to stay calm. I love you too, Sweetie. Help me out by being the great mother that you are. Please don't cry, Claire. It rips me up when you cry. I'll call as much as I can, and I'm always counting on you to give the kids hugs from Dad. Take a deep breath. One more, that's it.

"Hey, Hon, would it make you feel better about the boys if our company sponsored their team? They can use our KARS logo, and I'll pay for all of the team's uniforms. Maybe George could follow up on that for me; would you ask him? I'm glad that makes you pleased. And Claire, before I forget, let George know that the sky's the limit, as far as getting everything the kids need for their activities. Just have him use our charge card, and that goes for you, too, Claire. If there's something you need, or something I can do for you, that will make you cheer up. . . . Wait a minute. I know. You've been wanting a new sewing machine for your quilting. Why don't you get one? Get the top of the line. I know they're pricey, Sweetie, but I want you to have the best, because you're the greatest mom, and wife, that ever lived.

"I can still hear a few whimpers, Hon. I hate it when I make you cry like this, Claire. Honey, remember: deep breaths; we'll be together before you know it. I'll call you as soon as I'm settled in San Diego. Let me know if you want something else special, okay? Love you too. Bye."

Robert walked to the cooler in the corner of his office, and took a long drink, regrouping his thoughts, and allowing mental echoes of the phone call with Claire to slowly drain out of his mind. He heaved a sigh, took one more swallow, then crushed the cup in his hand and tossed it into the trash can. Leaning over to rest his arm on the cooler, he dropped his head down, gradually relaxing, as the chill of the water against his face helped him to unwind.

Soon he was dialing another familiar phone number, exhilarated when the soothing voice answered on the second ring. "Shelly, this is Robert," he said with self-assurance. "I want you to quit your job, and come with me for three weeks. I know it sounds crazy, but I'm serious. We're going to the coast for a week, then on to Vegas for at least two weeks, maybe more. And, when we return, I want you to move into my apartment. You don't have to work anymore, Shelly; I'm going to take care of you. Can you hurry and pack, then call Jim. Be sure and thank him from both us, okay?

"I love you too, Shelly. I know this is the happiest day of your life. One of mine, too."

It was hectic, going from his office back to his apartment to pack, then off to pick up Shelly, all in the short time he had. But she was ready for him, and she looked fantastic: white slacks, multi-colored silky blouse, with her gorgeous blonde hair falling freely to her shoulders. Her eyes were hidden behind sunglasses, but he could sense her gaze upon him, and felt like he had just won the lottery.

The couple stayed poised during the flight, just every day talk, while their hearts were accelerating with fervor, anticipating the unfolding of days ahead. After landing, they picked up their rental–a Mustang convertible–then drove to Coronado Island, where they would be staying for a week at the Hotel Del, a historic landmark since 1977. Shelly pinched her arm; she thought, for sure, as they drove across the bridge, and up the front drive of this charming castle, that she was in a fairy tale.

It was amazing to her how everyone rushed to take care of their needs. Robert had social status, and the attendees seemed to be aware of his elevated position. Once again Shelly pinched her arm. Yes, it was real. Grandma would turn over in her grave if she could see her granddaughter now. Come to think of it, she was probably watching over her, and that's how she ended up in such a beautiful fairy tale.

Other than the sound of waves hitting against the shore, the room was quiet, as the two of them unpacked, and freshened up. Then Robert walked to the open window, and gazed out at the breathtaking view of the ocean, the cool breeze whispering against his face. Shelly came up beside him, and took his hands in hers. "Robert, you have given me life again." His eyes looked down to gaze into her own. "I have existed for years, not really knowing if I would recognize what actual love is. My mother never had it; my father left as soon as she became pregnant. And my grandmother only gave her a superficial kind of love. So, to be loved by someone as wondrous as you is like finding my fairy tale, and being able to live it. I know I'm safe with you, Robert. Thank you for all that you have done for me in such a short time. I'm learning how to loosen up, for the first time in my life, and just be me."

Robert didn't have to hear anymore, and he definitely didn't want to say anything, for fear he would choke up. So he just took her hand, and led her out to the veranda, where they could watch the moon claim the night.

During the days that followed, while Robert was busy with work, Shelly took full advantage of her surroundings. She went to several museums, and other places of interest, her favorite being the Japanese Friendship Garden at Balboa Park, which was built in 1950. Within its confines, the spot she loved best was a sand and stone garden, with a bamboo pipe that filled with water until it tipped like a see-saw, spilling its contents over the rock below, and creating a sound meant to scare away evil spirits. Shelly felt assured that there were no evil spirits around her after being near the garden.

She also visited the Museum of Contemporary Art, located a few blocks from the beach in La Jolla, and overlooking the Pacific Ocean. The 60,000 square foot museum, with its magnificent costal views, was the region's foremost forum devoted to exploration and presentation of the art of the time, and Shelly was captivated by all of its history. She still wanted to be a teacher, so she loved hearing the lore of the area, soaking up all of the rich stories. Every day of the week she chose a different place to go, and in the evenings, if Robert wasn't too tired, they would continue to explore the region.

On one particular late afternoon they enjoyed snorkeling at La Jolla, where they were enthralled with the astonishing underwater view. Afterward they were pampered with a fantasy dinner under the moonlit sky. Shelly had several bruises on her arm where she'd continued to pinch herself, verifying that this was all actually happening. When Robert asked her how she had hurt herself, she smiled, and told him they were self-inflected.

"But why?"

"Because I keep thinking I'm dreaming."

On their last night there, they took a blanket and walked to the beach, to watch the sun set, and the moon rise. Shelly sat with her back braced against Robert's chest, his arms surrounding her waist, as he nibbled at her neck, and whispered softly in her ear, "Shelly, I want you to cease pinching yourself. I don't want to see any more bruises on your arms. What we have is for real, and it's going to prevail forever."

CHAPTER 18

Claire grasped Julie's hand, and with Davis, Eliza and Joey following behind, took lengthy strides, her ponytail flipping back and forth, as she advanced to the top bleachers, where Sam, Heather, Shannon and Tracy were already reserving their spots.

Sam's son, Paul Jr., was positioned at third base, while Claire's son Daniel was just getting ready to pitch.

"Hurry," Sam shouted, "You're going to miss Daniel's first pitch of the game."

Claire reached her destination, and quickly turned, her eyes following the ball as it crossed directly over the plate.

"Strike One," the umpire yelled.

"Good job, Daniel," hollered a husky voice, which Claire immediately recognized. "Now throw strike two."

"We want to sit with George," the children all cried in unison.

"We just got up here, Claire whined."

"I'll take them down, Claire," Heather offered with a smile. "I want to get closer, anyway, so I can give Daniel and Paul some encouragement; there's plenty of room by George."

Sam smiled. "Good idea, Heather; thanks for volunteering." Heather took Julie's hand, and while Davis called out to George, to make sure he knew they were coming to keep him company, the little tribe bounced their way down the bleachers, their feet plunking atop each wooden bench along the way.

Claire turned to Sam. "I was expecting to see Paul and Greg sitting with you and the other children," she observed.

"Long story." Sam heaved a sigh. "My husband and son are helping Kent Moulton, the owner of the mink farm, but not with their regular duties. It seems that Mr. Moulton's sister Audrey is moving from Idaho back to the farm, and needs help with the move. The way Mr. Moulton tells the story; he's relieved that she finally left her full-fledged drunk of a husband. Evidently, she's been through a very abusive marriage, and is finally getting divorced. She had no place to go, so Mr. Moulton talked her into moving back to Woodland, and living in their grandmother's home, just down the lane behind the mink barns. I'm sure it's going to need some sprucing up, and I plan to help out, but I'll wait until they move her in, and then take some warm homemade bread over, and make a survey of what I can do. Paul will undoubtedly fill me in on the details when he gets home tonight."

"Sam, I have such admiration for you. Sometimes I want to pinch you to see if you're real!" Claire paused. "Speaking of real, I have some crucial news. In fact, it's tremendous news!"

"What is it? Let me guess: Robert's moving back home."

"I wish it were that: Robert moving back home. It's not, but it's a close second." She grinned at Sam. "I'm pregnant!"

"What! You're what?"

"Shh, Sam. Everyone's looking at us. I don't want the whole town to know. Just you."

"Was this planned?"

"No, but I haven't been taking the pill, because Robert is gone more than he's home. I'm pretty sure I got pregnant on our fantastic Christmas trip."

"Oh, Claire, are you happy about this?"

"Yes."

"Then I'm happy too. Does Robert know?"

"Not yet. I'm going to call him tomorrow. He's just now arrived in Vegas, after being in San Diego for a week. He's working his head off, stressing out, trying to get these warehouses up and running. I'm so proud of his diligence, putting in long work days and nights. I worry about him overdoing, but he seems refreshed when I talk to him. By the way, did I tell you that George bought a boat?"

"No. When did he do that? Is it a big one?"

"Well, I kinda think Robert bought it for him, but I'm just guessing. George came over one day, a couple of weeks ago, and asked for Robert's phone number, for emergency calls. I gave it to him, thinking nothing of it. Then, a week later, he's knocking on the back screen door, really impatiently. I yelled out, 'I'm coming, I'm coming.' Well, he opened the screen, and said,

'You're not the quickest rabbit on the block. I ain't got all day! Where's the kids?'

"The next thing I knew, the kids were pushing each other, trying to be the first one out the door with George. I walked out, uninvited, and was shocked to see an eighteen foot Crest Liner boat in his drive way!

"'Well,' he said to me, 'I got a little something to take the kids out fishing.' Immediately I got nervous about them being out on a boat, but he reassured me they would be safe, and they would take classes before they actually went out. They named the boat, 'Time with Grandpa.'"

Sam grinned at Claire. "You are so blessed to have him around. How old is he, anyway?"

"He just turned seventy, but acts like he's fifty."

As the game came to its end, the two mothers screamed their excitement over the second victory, in a row, for the KARS baseball team. It had been a beautiful April spring day, but now there was a soft breeze coming from the north. Claire held her hand up to shade her eyes, noticing some dark clouds viciously moving their way. "We better hurry Sam; it looks like a storm is coming."

Sam grabbed the blankets from the bleachers, feeling the breeze, within minutes, whip up into a wind. "Do you have bad rain storms here? You're making me jittery."

"This time of year we have a few thunder storms, and they can be frightening. Let's hurry and round up the kids."

They found George huddled up with the children, and all ran together to their cars. George insisted on taking the young ones home with him to celebrate the win with Ethel's cookies and ice cream, and Claire ached with the knowledge that she and Robert should be hosting the event; they should be the ones to have the team over for cookies and ice cream. She sighed deeply. Why did she beat herself up with all the different scenarios and "what if's, always painting a picture in her mind that would never be complete? She turned, and sadly waved to the children as they drove safely away with George

As Claire pulled into her driveway thirty minutes later, having stopped to pick up a few grocery items at the Exchange, she noticed that the wind had already begun to wreak its havoc. The trash can by the side of the garage had blown over, and the screen door on the house was banging back and forth. She must have forgotten to close it tightly. She stepped from the car, balancing the two sacks on her hips. When the screen blew open again, she braced it with her body while she unlocked the door. Once inside, she set the sacks on top of the folding table by the washer, then went back outside to see if the kids had left anything in the yard that would blow away. The wind was getting stronger, and the whole area was darkened by storm clouds. Claire walked toward the lounge chair and rocker, both of which were tipped over, to recover them from the raging gusts.

The back yard was one of Claire's safe havens. It featured an old brick patio with a fireplace, and a play area for the children, accessed by a few stone steps leading down from the terrace. There were three trees that encircled the yard: a willow, from whose branches hung a tire swing, an apple, which boasted a hideout cabin that Robert had helped to build, and a large pine tree that–. Just then a loud crack sounded, as if the sky had broken apart, and the air around her reverberated with the boom of thunder. The rumbling slowly faded away with the dark clouds, but the lightening had hit the willow tree, splitting a heavy limb in two. Claire looked up just as the severed branch landed on her, forcing her to the ground, where she hit her head on some rocks. Within seconds another thunderbolt rolled over her, ricocheting throughout the area with a deafening roar. It was as if the devil, himself, stood over her, smiling at his victim!

Claire stirred, not knowing how long she had lain on the ground, and touched her forehead, feeling a bump, and drawing away bloody fingers. She pulled herself up, gathering her thoughts, realizing that lighting had hit the tree, which had, in turn, hit her. Though a little dizzy, she could stand, so she braced herself by resting her hand against the side of the house, then inched her way through the breeze-way, and into the back door.

She moved gingerly into the bathroom, and looked in the mirror, observing the huge bump on her forehead, as well as a gash by her eye, from which blood was oozing. She didn't think she needed stitches, just pressure. She started to cry, not only because she hurt, but because, for some reason, she'd really been missing Robert this entire, stupid day. She didn't believe that desiring comfort from her husband was a sign of weakness. It was just that, occasionally, she wished for his arms to be wrapped around her, letting her be the one to receive care, instead of the one always giving it. She knew she pretended a lot when the kids were around; it was important for them to believe that all was well. They certainly didn't want for anything; it was she, alone, who needed Robert's support.

Claire walked slowly into the kitchen for a glass of water, and when the phone rang, her heart skipped, hoping the call was from Robert. "Hello, hello. Are you still there?" asked the voice on the other end, after the initial greeting had stunned Claire into silence. She was groggy from the bump on her head, and puzzled over the caller's intent.

"Could you repeat that, please?"

"Well, like I said, I'm calling long distance from the Spring Mountain Clinic in Las Vegas, and I've been trying to reach Mr. or Mrs. Jensen."

Panic surfaced, as Claire listened to her words. "Is Robert okay? Has something happened to him?"

"No, no. That's not why I'm calling." The slightly agitated voice continued, "Mrs. Jensen, when you came in for your procedure, Mr. Jensen wrote out a check for the full amount owed. If I remember correctly, you were distraught, and he was being very attentive to you, and, in the process, he forgot to sign the check. Due to some confusion over phone numbers–he indicated that the one listed on the check was out of order–I've been going around in circles. The accounting department is breathing down my neck, wanting to get this matter resolved. Your husband did give me another number, which I tried, but the answering machine said I had called a Shelly Thompson. I'm very confused here; that's why I decided to try the number on the check, anyway, in hopes that the line had, in the meanwhile, been repaired.

"If you have a charge card, Mrs. Jensen, we could put the amount owed on that, and I will mail the unsigned check back to you. Would that be convenient?"

"Uh, yes. Just a minute; let me give you the number." Claire's hand was trembling as she rummaged through her purse, which was, fortuitously, sitting by the phone. "Okay, are you ready?"

"Yes, I'm here; go ahead." Claire read off the numbers.

"Thank you, Mrs. Jensen, and I hope you're feeling better. I know it was a rough day for you. I'll get your check in the mail first thing in the morning."

"Before you hang up," Claire's voice was shaking, "could you remind me of what medical procedure this payment covers?"

There was an awkward silence before the woman on the other end quietly whispered, "Mrs Jensen, it's for your abortion."

The receiver dangled from its cord, swinging back and forth, abandoned. Claire was on her knees, her head over the commode, retching, and trying to breathe at the same time. Eventually she was able to throw herself onto her bed, where she lay quivering from shock, nauseated by the word "abortion," and lonely, so very lonely.

CHAPTER 19

"Claire, Claire , where are you?" George had heard the lightning hit, and had taken the children to the basement with Ethel. Then, after checking the house and the kids for the second time, it dawned on him that the lightning must have hit close by. He walked to Claire's, and saw the huge split tree limb in the back yard, and blood in the breeze-way. His heart accelerated with the worry that he had waited too long, and the hope that Claire was okay.

Claire had cried herself to sleep, and though she was still groggy, she could hear her name being called, and feebly answered, "In my room." Her voice sounded unfamiliar to her, and fleetingly she wondered what was happening, before she again blacked out.

George walked into the bedroom, noticed that Claire was passed out on the bed, and immediately dialed 911. He then phoned Ethel, and asked her to make sure the kids didn't see the ambulance when it arrived. The paramedics pulled up to the house in minutes, and after indicating to George that Claire had a possible concussion, took her to the hospital to make sure everything else checked out. George promised to follow shortly to take care of admitting her, then made a third phone call, this one to Robert.

"Hello, this is Rob."

"Robert, this is George." His hand shook as he held the receiver, and his voice was jittery as he blurted out the words, "We've had a terrible storm here, and lightning hit the willow tree in your back yard, splitting it in half. Evidently, one of the branches hit your wife on the head. I called the ambulance, and they are taking her to the hospital for observation. Ethel's got the children, and I'm on my way up to get Claire checked in. She has a concussion, but I don't know what else, or how long she's been unconscious."

"George, I'm on my way. I'll call for the company plane, and be there in a couple of hours."

Claire slowly opened her eyes. She could hear voices, as well as the humming of machines.

As the doctor crossed to her bed, and took her hand, Claire's first impression was of how warm it was. "Where am I?"

The doctor gripped her hand as his words come out very softly, "Hi, Claire. My name is Doctor Burton, and I've been with you for the last four hours. You were hit on the head by a very big tree limb. Are you feeling nauseated, or dizzy?"

"Yes, I'm very dizzy."

"Okay Claire. I want you to relax. We're going to keep you for a couple of days, just to make sure the baby's okay."

Claire whimpered, "How did you know about the baby?"

"You told the parametrics in the ambulance, during a moment of consciousness."

"Is George here?'

"Yes, he's standing right behind me. I'm going to let you get some rest, but I'll.be here first thing in the morning to check on you. I want you to stay calm; can you do that for me?"

"Yes."

George stepped forward, taking the doctors place, tears running down his wrinkled cheeks. His words were gentle. "Ya give me a scare, Claire, so I'm glad to see ya awake. I don't want ya ta worry about the kids. Ethel and I will love 'em to pieces. I'm gonna go and let ya get some rest. I'm proud of ya, girl, for hangin' in there." His emotions were getting the best of him, and he didn't want to upset her more, so he leaned over and kissed her cheek. She could feel his tears.

"There's someone here that's been waitin' to talk with ya, so I'll be back in the mornin'. I love you, Sweetie."

"Love you, too"

George stood aside, and let Robert move in close. Claire noticed that his eyes were swollen and moist from the tears he had shed. As she stared at him, the memory of the phone call rushed back into her head, making a painful throbbing.

"I'm so sorry, Baby, so sorry I wasn't here to protect you." His voice was humble as he whispered the words, "I didn't know you were pregnant!" He rested his head next to hers, and put his arm over her, weeping convulsively once again, while repeating the words, "I'm so sorry."

Claire felt numb, but strong enough to whisper in his ear, "You need to leave, Robert. You need to go home and pack your bags, and leave."

His body stiffened, and he raised his head, looking into her eyes. "What are you saying,

Claire?"

"I'm saying that your choices have destroyed our family. I know about Shelly; I know about the abortion, and what it cost. After you get done packing, go over to George and Ethel's home, and tell your children goodbye." She gasped as if there were not enough air to breathe. Her face was wet with fresh tears, but her mind felt strong. "I'll get a lawyer, and have him contact you, and I pray to God that you will be man enough to support your children financially, so they won't have to suffer more than they already have."

He whispered, "What about the baby?"

"The baby will be my blessing. She's a fighter, and I love her for that."

"How do you know it's a girl, Claire?"

"I just know, and her name is Emma."

Robert stood, and looked down at Claire lying in the bed, so cherished by all who knew her. And here he was: a pitiful, sobbing man, trying to find a voice to utter his grieving words. "I am so sorry for hurting you and the children, so sorry, Claire." Then he walked toward the door, turning back long enough to declare, "I will make sure you are financially taken care of."

Claire wept convulsively, whimpering for God to please help her, help her to be strong for the children. As she finally felt herself drifting off, she was suddenly aware of someone lying by her side, gently cradling her, and whispering in her ear, "It's okay, my friend. I know what has come to pass, Claire, and I'll never leave your side. We'll get through this together. Now get some rest, my dear, dear, friend. Get some rest."

It was Sam.

CHAPTER 20

Robert's plane flew low over the Las Vegas strip, the lights beneath him crystallizing the view, almost as if you were looking into a glass music box, with little figures walking around to become a part of the scene.

It took just over an hour to travel from Woodland back to Vegas, his dwelling place for the past three weeks. The time in the air had become an uncomfortable, soul searching journey, with the thought of Claire lying in the hospital causing pain deep in his gut. In all likelihood, at the moment when the limb hit Claire on the head, he was in the hot tub, out on the balcony of the *Bellagio*, the posh hotel where he and Shelly had been in residence since leaving San Diego.

Claire knew about the abortion! How could she possibly have found out? Those incompetents at the clinic must have called his home for some reason, in spite of the fact that he'd made it very clear to them that the number on his check had been disconnected.

Shelly had begun suffering with morning sickness as soon as they'd left San Diego. There had been no doubt about her condition, and the only option the two of them could agree on was an abortion, so Robert took her to a recommended doctor in Vegas. Shelly wanted to continue school, and Robert felt that he was too old to start over again with a baby, or maybe he was just too selfish. Either way, a child, at this point, was out of the question.

And then there was Claire. If she did have a girl, like she so zealously claimed, that little girl would only think of him as one big jerk! Robert couldn't wrap his brain around the tremendous loss he would experience as his sons continued to grow older, and have families of their own. And his two–he gasped, and choked his emotions back down in order to carry on with his thoughts–his *three* little girls would never have respect for their slug of a father.

As the wheels of the plane hit the runway, jerking him back and forth for an instant, he made a promise to himself: for as long as he had money, he would make sure his children were taken care of. He knew, deep down in his heart, that the circumstances in which he now found himself, were according to the desires of his soul; he just didn't know how to deal with the hurt he had caused as a result. Nevertheless, he readily admitted that he was a selfish man, a working fool, and a toy boy, who felt trapped by his family. He reveled in the approval he received from those employed under him, as well as those who were over him, and he particularly took delight in his lover and playmate, Shelly.

A month later, Claire was still feeling jolted by the disaster of divorce, which had impacted and jeopardized the family. It would take a lengthy time for them, as a family unit, to recuperate. When Claire had told the boys that she was divorcing their father, they had simply shrugged their shoulders, protecting their hearts. The girls hung onto her for support, fearing what would happen if Daddy didn't take care of them.

Poor George, he stepped up to the plate, once again. He sat the children down in the living room, and explained to them the plan of survival: love each other, take care of each other, take the time for each other, and protect each other by continuing to be a strong family unit. Above all, communicate with each other their fears, feelings and needs.

He then took the boys aside, and talked with them, at length, about not boxing up their disturbing emotions. He told them that he would be available, twenty-four hours a day, to answer all of their questions. "You can trust me, boys; I'm here for you, and my job is to see that you become good, honorable men."

While George was thus engaged, Ethel and Claire gathered up the girls, and went out on the back patio, where they sat in the swings. "We want you girls to feel free to ask questions," Claire assured them. "The last thing Mommy wants is for you to be afraid. We will be a wonderful family, because we have George and Ethel to help us, as well as our other good friends. Mommy's going to need your help when the baby comes in September, and I want you to try really hard not to have fights with your brothers. "Are we okay? Do you have any questions?'

"Yes, Mommy, I have a question."

"What is it, Julie?"

"Well, every time Daddy got sad, I would give him butterfly kisses, and it made him feel better. But who's going to give him butterfly kisses now?"

Ethel looked at Claire, hoping she had the answer, because if she, herself, tried to speak, her words would be very shaky. Claire's first reaction to the question was a tendency toward a total melt down. Here this little girl's life was changing drastically, and she was worried that there would be no one to give her dad butterfly kisses. With her heart pounding inside of her, Claire silently prayed, "Please, God, don't let me come unglued right now." She took a deep breath, and motioned for Julie to come sit on her lap. "Julie, you can talk to your daddy, and let him know you will always have butterfly kisses for him, and I bet he will be very happy to know you still will share them."

"Okay, Mommy. Will you help me write him a note?"

"I'll be happy too."

Later that afternoon, while everyone was doing odd jobs, Claire could hear the birds chirping outside the open window. They'd found the birdhouse the boys had built with George, what seemed like forever ago. George had helped them hang it in the tree, and showed them where to put the feed. Now as the feathered creatures chirped their songs, Claire's heart filled with gratitude for friends who were willing to step into the role which Robert had abdicated.

"Mommy, I found some paper to write Daddy's letter."

Oh, my. Why had she thought that Julie would forget about the letter? Her young heart was too kind to ever forget about caring.

Dear Daddy,

mommy is helping me write this letter, (I know how to write, she is checking my words.)

I want you to know that at night when I say my prayers, I pray for you, even if you don't want us, I still want you. I hope you are happy Daddy, you did fun things with us, but the best fun thing was laying in the snow and sharing butterfly kisses. Daddy who is going to give you butterfly kisses when you are sad? I guess I could mail them to you.

Love,

Julie

p.s. we are going to have a baby sister, her name is Emma, her name means "all embracing" mommy said that means she's going to make our family circle *complete.*

P.p.s

Here is a butterfly kiss just because

With Julie's letter out of the way, Claire was in the mood to bake her apple pies for the Quilt Shop's bake sale, the proceeds of which would go toward the renovation of the library. Her mother was the professional pie maker, but had given Claire many tips and lessons before moving to Monterey, on the California coast, where she and Aunt Betty were heavily involved with the senior volunteer group. The climate there was temperate year 'round, so they did many outdoor activities, their favorite being to ride down the spectacular coastline, watch the sunsets, and gather seashells. In fact, her mom had invited her down for a week before the baby came in September, and before school started in the fall. Claire was hoping they could go the first of June, as soon as school was out for the summer.

The divorce was final, and each month a deposit was made to her account for support of the children. She'd never had a budget before, and, though she was inherently thrifty, she was also used to splurging once in a while. Now, judging by the amounts being transferred from Robert's bank into hers, she was going to have to tighten her spending considerably. She snickered to herself, thinking how nice it would be if Robert would give her an open check book. Wouldn't that be a trip? But no such luck. By the time she paid the house and car payments, and bought groceries, whatever pennies were left over had to be sufficiently pinched.

She knew Robert made more than he claimed, but with him living out of state, he was able to hide it somehow, and her lawyer couldn't find any evidence to support her contention. The settlement was fair in Robert's eyes, and his lawyers seemed to be from the James Bond Series: all-important, assertive and abrasive. She knew she couldn't afford to fight him, so she would soon have to find work, but dreaded the thought.

Her mother and Aunt Betty had offered to help pay for their flights, when the time came, plus George and Ethel were going to join them, to assist with the children. She wistfully wished that Robert would kick some bonus money her way for good behavior. "Whatever," she laughed to herself. One thing she was certain of: she wouldn't be the one getting bonuses for good behavior; it would be Robert's playmate. Nevertheless, Claire knew her family all needed a break, and was determined that they would somehow make this trip. It had been a horrendous, life-changing year.

With the apple pies baking in the oven, Claire decided to hurry and mop the floors, while the children were outside, playing on the trampoline. They had six more weeks of school, so Saturdays were definitely play days.

As she was pulling out the pies, the boys crept up behind their mother to surprise her. That they did! As they, in unison, screamed "Boo," the apple pie she had in her hands tilted, and crashed to the clean, just-mopped linoleum. The boys stiffened, dreading her response, and were very surprised when she flumped to the floor, laughing. "It's a good thing the floors are clean," she giggled. "Grab some forks, and join me down here. We'll see if these are worthy of the bake sale." Quickly overcoming their initial shock over her reaction, they joyously joined her, unanimously agreeing to make sure the next pie in the oven made it safely to the bake sale, while their forks dipped into the apple pie, now apple turnover, being served from the floor.

CHAPTER 21

George came clambering in through the back door with an album in his hands, calling the boys names. "We're in here, George, on the floor. Don't ask; just grab a fork, and join us."

"What ya got, George?" Daniel said in between bites, as their neighbor seated himself, took a fork-full of pie, and opened the album across his lap.

"Look, Daniel," Davis pointed, "it's a picture of an old truck."

"Yeah, it's really old," piped in Joey.

"Yes, my little rug rats, it is that. It's old, but still running, kind of like me. But it does need some work done to bring it up to snuff."

"What's 'snuff'?" Joey's nose was crinkled as he directed his question to his grownup pal.

"You know, freshen it up, get it ready for you boys to drive."

"What?" Daniel squealed. "It's for us to drive? How cool is that, Mom?"

"That's way cool, Son. Now I'll clean this up while you boys look at the pictures." Then, as George and the boys stood, she added, "Wait a minute. Don't leave. I can't get up; I think I'm stuck." They all offered her their hands at once, pulling her to standing position.

Daniel grinned. "Hey, Mom, do you need help getting the next pie out of the oven?"

Claire smiled back at him. "No, I know how to take a pie out of the oven. The second time is always the good luck charm, and my preference would be to do it alone, with no booing. Now skedaddle, scamper, leave. I have a floor to clean . . . again!"

George took the boys way out to the far west end of his property, where stood a ramshackle garage. Taking a key from his pocket, he inserted it into the rusty old lock attached to the weathered door, and popped open the shank. The boys felt like they were on a treasure hunt, and when George opened the doors, they all gasped. There sat a sharp 1950 V8 Ford truck. George smiled. "Well, boys, we have our work cut out for us, but as a team, we can have it running in no time. Are ya with me?" The boys began jumping up and down, and George had to brace himself against the truck as they swarmed in with their hugs, and pats on the back for saving them, once again, from the reality caused by their father's choices.

Claire made her way, step by step, up to the Quilt Shop door, carefully balancing the one surviving pie. As she reached for the door knob, she noticed the sign, **FOR SALE.** What? Mrs. Murray was selling the Quilt Shop? No way! Why, Sam hadn't mentioned a word about it. Once inside, she made her presence known by speaking in a loud voice to Mrs. Murray, "You can't sell this shop. What will we do? This has become my addiction of choice!" Gasping for air, only partially due to the pregnancy, she continued in a dither, "I'll die without fabric and bonding."

"Claire, calm down. Let me help you with this delicious looking pie. Now there, I'll take it before you drop the whole thing on the floor, and I'll just set it over here until we have everything gathered for the bake sale." Mrs. Murray drew in a deep breath, and slowly exhaled, running her hands slowly over her pink flowered cotton dress, as if she were ironing it: a habit to which she yielded, when she needed time to think. "You've got me in a tizzy, Claire.

"Now the answer to your question is: I'm selling the shop, not closing it. I met this wonderful gentlemen at the Seniors' Dance, and we can't leave each other alone. He brightens my day, and I do the same for his. But, he wants to buy a big motor-home and travel. Now, who could say 'no' to that?"

"No one could say no to such a nice proposal. I'm sorry for ruffling your feathers. It's just, well, it's just that I love this shop; it's my safe haven."

"Then why don't you buy it, Claire? You would be good at assisting people, and with Sam by your side, you couldn't lose. Plus, you could bring your baby with you every day. The possibilities for this little shop would be endless, with a younger owner like yourself."

Claire's mouth was wide open, her mind running a mile a minute. "Is Sam here?"

"Yes, she's in the classroom."

Sam was leaning over her drawing board, her back to the door, as she concentrated on illustrating the proper technique for making fabric points come together. Claire began to verbally ramble, in true motor-mouth fashion, as if Sam were already aware of her close proximity. "Sam, if I bought this shop, would you always be the teacher, and be by my side through thick and thin, continue this crazy path we're on, called life, but surviving by doing something we love, we might even make some money?"

92

Sam's jaw dropped as she stood, and turned to face her friend. "Claire, that's the best idea you've had for a long time. Let's do it, Girlfriend." They approached one another, Sam jumping up and down, and Claire trying to, but knowing her efforts weren't as effective as Sam's. So they hugged, then hugged again, and then hugged some more.

"Oh," Claire sighed, "one slight problem; I have no money."

They both started laughing. "Yeah, that is a problem."

Claire rolled her shoulders back. "Never fear, Sam. I'm on a mission to make this my Quilt Shop, so help me God." Then she whispered to herself, "And, God, will you please help me?"

Claire had a lengthy talk with George about the prospect of owning the Quilt Shop. He was very supportive, and offered financial help, but she told him that he already spent enough of his retirement money on her and her family. She would approach Aunt Betty for help in obtaining a loan, and with the possible offer of a partnership. Going to her bedroom for privacy, she dialed her aunt's number.

Everything she proposed, Aunt Betty supported one hundred percent. It was agreed that they would secure a bank loan in Claire's name, with Aunt Betty, who was delighted at the opportunity to help her niece, as co-signer. Next, Claire went back to the shop, and asked Mrs. Murray to take down the sign, then she headed for the bank.

With so much to do, Claire had to cancel the trip to California to visit her mother, but promised the children they would absolutely go next year, which would be more fun, because the baby would be with them by that time. She then turned her efforts toward the task at hand.

It took a few weeks to obtain the loan, and arrange the closing, but soon Sam and Claire were sitting on the floor of the newly acquired Quilt Shop, sprawled out with a variety of books surrounding them. They were choosing what classes Sam could teach, and filling out the order sheets for the notions. Plus, they were considering, and checking out the possibility of selling sewing machines.

They had been busy for hours, planning door prizes, and putting together a class schedule for their customers, who would receive a discount for signing up on the day the doors opened under the new management. They had also painted a sign for the front window:

Grand Opening, Sept. 27th.

Claire made a tooting noise through an empty Scott towel holder. "Hear ye, hear ye. Presenting the newfangled, pregnant owner, Claire Jensen. And right next to her, sitting Indian style on the floor, dressed in her cut-offs, and white embroidered cotton blouse, is the number one, most talented teacher in the history of quilt shops, the one and only Samantha Rose Parker. Take a bow, Miss Parker." Sam jumped up and took an over exaggerated bow. "Is there anything you would like to say to your loyal fans?"

"Yes, I would like to say, 'come walk with me down memory lane.'"

"Oh, gag, Sam, that wasn't very creative."

Then Sam fell to the floor, poking fun at Claire. "You don't think I'm creative, huh? Just for that I'm gonna get on my black stallion, and ride off into the sunset."

Oh, give me a break. Hey, Sam, I wonder if Robert's ditsy new playmate is as creative as I am? I mean, I can't imagine why he would want her over me." Claire was giggling so hard she couldn't breathe. "Just look at me! I'm one big pregnant woman, dying for romance, sitting on the floor, eating M&Ms, and drinking my diet Coke with my cohort. What's that song we sing all the time? Oh, yeah. *It's simple and it's plain, why should I complain, but tell me, does she kiss like I used to kiss you? Da da da da.* Sam stood and danced to Claire's singing, until Claire stopped abruptly. "Sam, my water just broke!"

Within minutes Sam had Claire to the hospital, where the nurses greeted them as they pulled into the emergency drive-through. Carol and Glenna, the attending nurses, had been with Claire in every delivery, and she was relieved to see they were both on duty. As they began to prepare her for delivery, Carol announced that, "Doctor Pitts is on his way."

Sam immediately took over her duties as delivery room coach, wiping Claire's forehead with a cool cloth, timing the contractions, and whispering encouraging words, while letting her friend dig into her arm as the contractions become stronger. Soon Doctor Pitts walked into the room with his sterilized, gloved hands in the air. "Okay, Claire, let's get the little girl here we've been talking about."

Within the hour Claire heard a cry, and Sam began jumping up and down, squealing, "It's her, Claire. It's Emma."

Almost simultaneously she heard Doctor Pitts saying, "Here is little Emma, and she is beautiful." Emma weighed eight pounds, six ounces, and had dark curly hair all over her head. It was obvious that her lungs were in excellent condition, as she let everyone know she had arrived.

Sam leaned over Claire, wiped away her tears, and kissed her cheek, then whispered in her ear, "Good job, Girlfriend. I'm proud of you."

Claire didn't want anyone to call Robert; she felt that he had relinquished all his rights of fatherhood, and that Emma was hers alone. George and Ethel brought the kids up to see their new sister, and, of course, promised to keep the little Munchkins until Claire was released. After everyone left, Claire called her mother to give her the news. Finally, in the quiet of her room, in the still of the night, she thanked God for all her blessings, then wept some more.

Robert had been calling the house, but couldn't get an answer, so telephoned George around nine that night, and was informed that they had all been at the hospital, seeing the new baby. Robert become very quiet, then asked, "Was it a girl, like Claire said it would be?"

"Oh, yes, a beautiful little girl."

Suddenly Julie was by George's side. "Is that my daddy?" George nodded his head. "Can I talk to him?" George told Robert he had someone who wanted to say hello.

"Daddy, this is Julie. Oh, Daddy, I have a beautiful little sister, and Mommy said I could help watch her, and if she cries, I can give her my butterfly kisses. So, Daddy," Julie became timid, "I don't have any more butterfly kisses for you, because you don't want us, but my baby sister needs me now."

With tears in her eyes, she handed the receiver to George. "Here, George, I don't want to talk anymore."

George took the phone, trying to hold back his own tears. "Are you still there?"

Robert replied listlessly, "George, just so you know, I recognize that I made the biggest mistake of my life leaving my family." His voice was tender, his words slurred with emotion. "I'm so selfishly stupid."

CHAPTER 22

Claire locked the door of the Quilt Shop, reached to the window and turned the sign to closed, then, while Sam straightened and refolded the fabric bolts, she walked to the thread rack, and started putting the colors back in their proper places. The store actually looked like a hurricane had hit it, but it was the best storm either one of them could have anticipated. They hadn't counted the register yet, but Claire knew one thing for sure: they would definitely be able to pay off some huge fabric shipments.

Sam crossed the room and wrapped her arms around Claire's shoulders. "It's going to work, Claire; we are going to have a hopping store. I can feel it. And there was nothing but positive comments about the way we revamped the fabrics, how we have given it a country look, and made space for another classroom. I want to live here, I love it so much. It is the warmest, kindest, safe haven I've had the privilege of being in for a very long time. And to think I've contributed to something so peachy! It just makes me smile."

"I feel the same way, Sam. With Christmas coming, and all the fun opportunities we will be offering for the holidays, our little store will be on the map. I was thinking, Sam, about a 'Quilt 'Til You Wilt' class, but it would have to be an all-nighter. What do you think?"

"Claire, how clever! I'll put that in the newsletter. I also want to add a class on color and design, plus one on the darling new Christmas tree skirt. So let's count." Sam stuck up a finger for each item as she named them. "Applique, Stars, Running Geese, Beginners, and Color & Design, plus the 'Quilt 'Til You Wilt' night. That's a pretty good lineup to start off with, and then we can talk to Clara Barnes to see if she is still interested in teaching."

Claire sighed, "Everything seems so right; don't you think, Sam?"

"Yes, everything seems so right," she repeated.

Two years slipped away, gliding by as smoothly as possible for a single mom with six active youngsters. The children absolutely catered to baby Emma's every need and desire. Julie and

Eliza never let her lack for attention, while the boys just pampered her constantly, as if she were a delicate doll. Little Emma knew how to pull the strings, and melt the hearts of her siblings.

The family had never made the promised trip to California. Claire found that it took an inordinate amount of her time, just to figure out how to fit her family, her work, and all of the children's activities into a routine that worked for them. It was like putting a puzzle together, trying to make every little piece of their life fit just right.

Nevertheless, school was out, once again, and this was the time for them to take a much needed break. Daniel was eighteen, and had just graduated, with high grades and the possibility of several scholarship opportunities. That was another good reason for a trip: celebrating his accomplishments. He loved working on cars, especially with George, and had learned a great deal while restoring the old Ford truck that he now shared with Davis. He hoped to increase his skill in reviving antiques cars. As no surprise to Claire, he had continued a relationship with Sam's daughter Heather all through high school.

Davis, just finishing his junior year, was a devoted basketball player for the Woodland Wasps, and was wrapped up in football, as well. Anything athletic held his interest, and when he participated, he was one hundred percent dedicated. He had a following of girls, who were not only attracted by his sports abilities, but also by the debonair looks he had acquired from Robert. When he smiled his dimpled smile, they melted.

Eliza was Claire's biggest worry. She was extremely boy crazy, and very forward in her thoughts. Many of her actions caught Claire off guard. The best description would be: she was Claire's wild child.

The house two doors down from them had stood vacant for a year, but was recently purchased by a middle-aged couple, who turned it into a half-way home for troubled kids. At first, Claire didn't give it a second thought. Then she noticed, several times, that Eliza was hanging out with one of the boys who lived there, a black boy. He was teaching her behaviors that were troubling to Claire, but when she expressed her motherly concerns to Eliza, the girl pretended to listen, and then, as soon as Claire left for work, she did what she wanted.

Claire was at the shop a good percentage of each day, as well as on some evenings, to help with the quilting classes. Now that the children were getting older, they were able to fend for themselves in her absence. However, each time she walked in through the door, they would all start at once, letting her know who did what, and who didn't follow the work sheet she'd left. It was a race, seeing who could rat on the other ones first.

Joey, thirteen, was a mama's boy; he did nothing to cause contention, just went with the flow. He was handsome, very witty, and Claire's right-hand man. She felt a deep affection for this son.

Julie was Claire's little fireball. She just wanted everyone to be happy, and had proclaimed herself as Emma's number one caretaker. It was like playing with dolls for her, only this one was her real live sister, to whom she never tired of giving butterfly kisses.

George was now seventy-three, and Ethel wasn't far behind. He had helped the boys refurbish the truck which they now shared, and he still took them out fishing, but had begun to pull back dramatically as they grew older.

Claire seldom heard from Robert; she did know that he and Shelly were still together, but not married. Claire couldn't imagine ever dating again, let alone re-marrying. Who would want to take on the responsibility of such a large family as hers? She felt she was hardly worth the hassle. She had nothing to give, and no one could ever love her children like she did. It wasn't worth the sweat to even let her thoughts dribble in that direction.

Claire and Sam had, by now, hired a new employee, Clara Epperson, and really felt like they had hit the jack pot. She was not only exceptional with customer service, but was completely trustworthy, and very capable of managing the shop on her own. This gave Claire and Sam the opportunity to take a proposed jaunt to California together. Clara was also very talented at the art of crocheting, and wanted to incorporate these lessons with the list of quilt classes.

It had been decided that the two families would take a coastal trip together. Claire and Sam would visit some fabric mills while there, killing two birds with one stone, and making it possible for them to use their traveling expenses as a tax write-off.

Sam was antsy as she anticipated the well deserved vacation. As always, she was busy searching for new ideas for the Quilt Shop, but, in addition, she had some concerns about her husband Paul. He had declined the offer to join them, saying he was really tied down on the mink farm, and, when he started stuttering with jumbled reasons for staying behind, Sam was overcome with foreboding. Her heart pulsated, telling her that something was not right, but she didn't have the time, right then, to play detective with him. She would deal with it when she returned home.

Her oldest son Greg had joined the navy, and was stationed at the Naval Training Center in San Diego, but, unfortunately, Sam wouldn't be able to visit him during their trip, as he was still in recruit training.

Paul Jr. had graduated with Daniel, also with flying colors, so this trip was a double celebration. And, with Heather and Daniel being in a strong relationship, life was like a beam of light shining down on the three of them.

Shannon, fourteen, and Tracy, twelve, were both timid, compared to Eliza, and weren't too chummy with her. Julie, being quite a bit younger, had little in common with the older girls, but usually just went with the flow, her priority being baby Emma.

Sam and Claire knew there might be a few rumblings between the girls, but hoped that they would learn to relax with one another, and take advantage of making some great memories. They were also thankful that George and Ethel had agreed to come. George would definitely keep the boys entertained.

Their flight took off as scheduled, and Emma thought she was on cloud nine, with all the attention she received from the flight attendants. One of them commented on how much she looked like Shirley Temple, and, even though Emma had no clue who that was, she loved all of the pampering given to her tiny little self.

They landed safely at Limburg Airport, in San Diego, where a driver was waiting to take the families to Humphreys Half Moon Inn, to begin their week's stay. Claire was thrilled that her mother and Aunt Betty would soon be joining them there. Humphreys was located on Shelter Island–San Diego's own Hawaiian Isle–framed by America's Cup Harbor and San Diego Bay. It was a tropical resort-style hotel, offering breathtaking views, and just minutes away from the local attractions.

After everyone was settled in their rooms, and welcoming hugs were given to Grandma Grace and Aunt Betty from all the children except the youngest one, Claire carried in her grandmother's little namesake, Emma, whom she had held back until the group quieted down. "Mother, Aunt Betty, I would like to introduce you to our little miracle, and the light of our lives."

Little Emma surprised Claire as she extended her arms toward Grandma Grace, saying, "Mama, mama." Claire had shown her pictures, and often let her telephone her mother, but this was a particularly affectionate debut for all who observed it. Everyone pampered Emma for awhile, by playing into her unique personality, but soon they were ready to hang out, and discover their surroundings. Thus the week-long vacation began.

Once they'd had a good night's rest, the adventures commenced. It started with George taking all the boys sports fishing, while the women folk and girls built sand castles, did some shopping, and then waited for George to bring the fishermen back, so they could go to Sea World.

Subsequent days went kind of like this: much food consumption, Legoland, Old Town Trolly, diving, snorkeling, some fighting between teens, maybe a little too much hugging by other teens, little sleep, sunburns, Point Loma's Historial Site (George kept them educated), rides on the authentically restored flying horse carousel, trying to keep Eliza away from boys, trying to keep Eliza dressed modestly, USS Midway Carrier Museum (that would be George again, giving them more history), and Belmont Park Amusement Center, with all tempers and moods still reasonably intact.

Then Sam and Claire toured the fabric mills for one whole day, checking out all of the newest fabrics that would be hitting the market in the fall. There was also a fabric convention in downtown San Diego, where all of the distributors had booths with the latest notions, patterns, and fabric. Everything the two women saw would be great for the shop, and the temptation was almost impossible to resist, but Sam and Claire worked hard at being very selective.

They were dead tired, or better words would be pooped out, when they returned to the resort. Needless to say, all the teens and the younger ones were still going full thrust, out on the beach. But little Emma was asleep on Claire's bed, with Grandma Grace enjoying a late nap. They would be leaving in the morning, but what a wonderful, eventful, and bonding vacation this had become. The memories they'd made would last for a very long time.

After deciding upon an ice cream night at the Del Coronado Hotel, they all boarded the public transit, and traveled over the Coronado Bridge to the acclaimed landmark, where the waitress had to rearrange many tables in order for that many to sit together in a circle. The Del Coronado lived up to all expectations, and they listened intently as George shared the history of the place while they devoured their ice cream. "The Hotel del Coronado has a rich and colorful heritage that sets it apart from neighboring hotels, especially in regards to the ghost Kate Morgan."

"A ghost!" screamed Julie.

There was a general hubbub as they teased and laughed over the idea of a ghost. But even above the commotion from their own group, they were disturbed by a woman's loud laughter. From their seats around the table, where they were slurping up the remains of the melting ice cream cones, the entire lighthearted family turned in unison to see who had such a raucous laugh. They watched as the man standing behind her spanked the woman on her rear, then raised his head to advance in their direction. At that moment, his dimpled smile froze, as he beheld his former neighbors, his ex-wife, ex-in-laws, and his children, looking amazed and shocked at their father and his girlfriend.

CHAPTER 23

George arose from his seat at the family table, walked over to the stunned and unmoving Robert, and whispered to him, "Let me escort you and your friend out." They turned in unison, and went back out the door that, just a few seconds before, the couple had so unwarily entered.

George walked them down the hall to the end of the building, then turned to look Robert in the eye, his voice low-toned and stern. "This is an unfortunate calamity, Robert. Your family has been coping with their new reality, and after a lotta unified effort, they've just enjoyed an outstanding retreat from some pretty harsh times. This was a family gathering, celebrating new horizons, like Daniel's graduation, as well as Paul, Junior's. How does that make ya feel, Robert?"

"I . . . I'm speechless." He then turned to Shelly, and placed his hand on her shoulder. "I need you to go back to our room, and give me some time."

With tears in her eyes, she nodded. "I'm so sorry, Mister–"

"It's just George, ma'am. Just call me George."

"I'm sorry, George. We had no idea." She then turned, her steps quickening as she made her way toward the front entrance of the Del Coronado.

George looked at Robert. "Wha'd'ya wanna do, Robert?"

Robert couldn't control the quaver in his voice as he replied, "I would like to meet with my family for a few minutes, if they will let me."

With George's hand on Robert's shoulder they walked back inside, as George gave silent thanks for the lateness of the hour; there were few customers in the shop other than the family group. George looked at each one of them, still keeping his arm firmly around his shamefaced companion. "Robert would like to visit with his family, if you feel comfortable with that. If that's not an option you're okay with, then he'll understand your feelings."

It was deadly quiet for what seemed like an eternity, before Julie piped up, and said, "Daddy,

102

do you want to meet Emma?"

Robert's eyes circled the table; he had forgotten, for a split second, that he had a child he had never seen. As his eyes traveled around the group, they landed on a beautiful little girl, with dark curly hair, and huge blue eyes. Julie lifted Emma out of her high chair, then carried her over to her Father. "Daddy, this is our little Emma. Isn't she just the cutest little girl you've ever seen?"

Robert smiled at Emma, then extended his arms toward her, forcing George's hand to slip from his shoulders. Emma responded with no hesitation, and Robert gasped as his little precious child put her tiny arms around his neck, and hugged him. He thought he would pass out from all of the turmoil that was building up inside of himself. Tears streamed down his face, as the little girl remained cuddled against his chest, her hug unbroken.

All of the family sat quietly immovable, as they witnessed a miracle of forgiveness. Julie had presented the way, and Emma was the miracle. There was not a dry eye in the place; even the manager had turned to watch the scene that was playing out. He'd been worried that there would be family contravention, and was relieved to observe the warmth that had been extended to the man standing with a child's arms wrapped around his neck.

Within minutes, Robert was unanimously invited to sit with them. After Sam's family were introduced, they excused themselves, so the others could have some private time with Robert. She whispered to Claire that they would take a taxi back to Humphreys, then each of them hugged or patted Robert on the shoulder, encouraging him to enjoy his time.

Daniel instructed Heather to stay behind, so that he could let his father know about their future plans. Then, one by one, the children told their father about their personal goals. Not everyone was delighted about the situation to which they'd been consigned. Eliza was jittery when it came her turn to talk to her dad. With disgust openly displayed upon her face, and with a beady-eyed stare, she said, "I really don't have anything good to say about my life." Then she stood, and ran out the door.

Davis looked at his mother, and whispered, "I'll go get her, and walk her back to our taxi." Claire was thankful for her son's actions, and, since they had all now had the chance to talk to their father, she suggested they head back to Humphreys, because of the early flight out in the morning. They all agreed, and began to make their way out of the ice cream shop, while Claire apologized to the manager, and thanked him for his patience.

Once back at the hotel, the children give their father a hug, and said their goodbyes. Claire had asked Julie to get Emma ready for bed, and put her in the crib, as soon as they returned to the resort, so Julie now smiled, and immediately left with her baby sister. Making every minute count, Emma waved to them with her little hand, and flashed her attention-getting smile, as she faded out of view.

Robert asked Claire if she would like to sit for a while on the bench that overlooked the ocean, and as they gazed out at the full moon dancing over the rolling waves, Claire's weakened voice broke the silence. "I heard you talk to Daniel about a position with KARS."

"Yes, we're expanding the warehouse in Salt Lake, and he would be a good candidate. I think he's a shoo-in." Robert smiled that smile that melted her insides, just as it always had. "I have a certain amount of pull with the boss."

"I appreciate the offer, Robert. I'm sure there will be a wedding in the fall."

"Don't worry, Claire, I will make sure they have the wedding they hope for."

"Thank you, Robert." Her heart felt like it had stopped beating, but she continued, "Are you happy?"

Robert stiffened beside her. "The truth?"

"Yes, the truth."

"No, I'm not what you'd call happy. I live for my work, as you well know, but you would be surprised at how many nights I can't sleep. I'm miserable, just thinking about how badly I've messed up. I know this sounds cruel, but Shelly is someone who is there for comfort. If I had my wishes, I would still be married to the girl of my dreams, who has given me five beautiful children, and a baby angel." His words ricocheted through Claire's heart, making her tremble. "Is it to late, Claire? Is there any way you could forgive me?"

His words left Claire frozen with shock and regret. Turning to look at those deep blue eyes, and that adored dimple in his cheek, she felt like she had been catapulted back in time to the night he appeared on the hill, and swept her off her feet. Taking a deep breath, she replied, "Yes, Robert, it's too late. I don't know how to start mending my heart, but I must. I could never trust you again; I would always question every move you made. But I hope you will keep in contact with your children. They love you so unconditionally, Robert, and rightly so. Eliza is the one I worry most about. She has kept all of her anger over the divorce bottled up inside, and I fear I can't provide her with all of the answers."

Robert heaved a sigh, then knelt before Claire, as if to beg. "Are you for sure about us,

Claire? Can't you please forgive me? Reach out to me, Baby. Take a chance on us, for the children. I still love you, Claire!"

"Robert, don't! Don't throw the children into this. You knew that your choices, or addictions, or whatever it is that you can't control, is why we're where we are today. Don't you dare put this back in my lap. I've been trying to hold this family together for two years, and just because you've seen us, you want to start all over, like nothing has happened. How do you do that?"

He stood, grabbed her shoulders, and said, "This is how you do that." Then, pulling her up against him, he kissed her hard, and possessively.

Breaking his hold, she ran down the stone walkway to the bus stop, and braced herself against the light pole, hoping a bus would come soon. Then, fearing her own emotions, she waved down a taxi, instead. She had to get away quickly; otherwise, she might give in to her longings, and turn to run back to Robert.

CHAPTER 24

"Let's sit over there. Hurry! Snatch the seat before that lady gets it."

Sam bolted to the two empty seats, three rows back from the screen, and directly in the center of Woodland's popular Ideal Theater.

"Good girl," Claire said in a soft mumble, continuing down the aisle. Heads turned as she measured each step, not wanting to trip in the aisle, and splatter their pizza all over the floor. Sam and Claire couldn't imagine anything more comforting than pizza, and Tom Cruise.

The cartoons covered the screen first, so the two of them had time to chill out, and become less uptight after a busy day at the shop. They groaned with pleasure over each bite of pizza, and every sip of their icy cold Cokes. People sitting nearby grumbled over the idea of bringing pizza into the movie house, but, as far as Claire and Sam were concerned, there was no sign saying, "NO PIZZA ALLOWED."

Claire glanced to one side, and noticed two older men, sitting a couple of seats over, staring at them. She leaned across, and asked them if they would like a piece of pizza, then rolled her eyes at Sam, but was taken by surprise when the answer was, "Yes." Claire passed it over to them, and included a napkin, to boot.

Sam sank down in her seat, nudging Claire. "I hope they don't think we're hitting on them."

Claire started laughing as she replied, "Girlfriend, that's exactly what they're thinking. But tonight our hearts belong to Tom," she said loudly enough that the two older gentlemen could hear her.

The movie began, and Sam and Claire were soon spellbound by Tom Cruise and Kelly McGillis. Wow! How would it be to ride behind a jock on a motorcycle, holding on extremely tightly, and traveling down the coast by the naval base?

After recovering from that scene, they clutched fake mikes in their hands, and sang, "You've

106

lost that loving feeling, whoa, whoa, that loving feeling." They pretended not to hear the "Shh"s, and "Be quiet"s. They were one hundred percent into this movie, and, as far as they were concerned, it was a great escape; they were in their own little world.

When the movie ended, the two friends, with their tear stained faces, continued to sit. "Are you thinking what I'm thinking?" said Sam.

"Yes. Here's my money for another ticket, and, while you're up, get us some chocolate."

Shortly after midnight, at the conclusion of the second showing, they slowly sauntered to the park across the street from the theater. The little town was quiet, and it was a warm summer night, so they lazily strolled to a park bench, and sat down, each one a little mellowed by the movie. Leaning back, and stretching her legs out, Claire looked at Sam. "Are you okay?"

"Yeah, I'm okay. But it was nice, just being taken away from reality for a while."

"Our world isn't that bad, is it Sam? After the confrontation with Robert, on our trip, I didn't think I would recover. But, thanks to you, and your unconditional support, I've been able to put my life in perspective. It's a real crazy one, but it's mine to keep. I owe you so much, Sam, for keeping my head above water when I thought I was drowning."

"You don't have to thank me, Claire. We've known, from the first time we met, that we must have been friends long before we come to earth. Our connection, and value, to one another is a bond that was made in heaven. With God's grace He has let us continue our journey together, and if one of us, heaven forbid, leaves this world before the other, whoever it might be will be waiting to greet the friend she left behind."

Claire placed her arm around Sam's shoulder. "If I go first, Sam, I'll thank God for the two of us."

Audrey Spens parted the lace curtains that covered her front window, to see if Paul was coming up the path. She resented the necessity of starting her life over again, but couldn't continue to submit to the constant physical and emotional abuse rendered by her ex-husband, and was relieved when Kent, her brother, assisted her in breaking loose from her bondage. He'd had no idea of her circumstances, until she finally escaped and called him. Kent had just assumed that she wanted nothing to do with him after their parents died, but he was totally wrong, and was shocked to find out the truth: that she was not allowed to make contact with him.

Audrey had become a victim a little over a year after she was married, when it became apparent that, if she didn't obey her husband's every command, she had reason to fear for her life.

107

He had beaten her, off and on, for the past five years, or more. Now, at the age of thirty-five, she had found sanctuary in her grandmother's old home, owned by her brother. She felt safe here, and even safer in the arms of Paul Parker.

Sam knew Paul was spending a lot of time "helping Audrey," as he put it. It was just like every other place they'd ever lived. Paul would zoom in on a woman, desperate and alone. Then, when he got in over his head, his family would have to move. Sam never let on that she knew he was a deceiver, or should she say a trickster? Whatever the description, her plan was to look the other way until the children were gone. She didn't care about herself, but, unlike Claire, if she left Paul, she would have to go into hiding, for fear of retaliation. Paul had never yet abused her, but he thought he owned her. She just needed to hang on until Tracy graduated, which was three more years.

CHAPTER 25

The diamond that Daniel had purchased for Heather was beautiful, and the wedding would take place the end of the month; June 29, 1988 was printed on the invitations. Daniel had taken the job his dad had offered him at the new KARS distribution center in Salt Lake City, where he was training to be supervisor within the year, and would be a huge asset to the company. He had an apartment up in the Avenues, and was doing very well, putting his money aside, so he could buy a new home for his bride-to-be.

She was part of the Woodland graduating class of 1988, receiving high honors, and planning, once they were settled, to attend the University of Utah's medical school. Though it drove Daniel crazy being away from her, she was definitely worth the wait.

Daniel had talked to his dad several times, inviting him to the wedding, but Robert had declined, his excuse being that he didn't want to cause Claire any uneasiness. George was the man standing in his place, next to Claire, and rightly so. Therefore, Daniel was taken by surprise when Robert told him to send him the bill; that was the least he could do for his son.

Daniel's brother was honored at being asked to serve as best man. Davis was graduating with the same class as Heather, and had received a scholarship to a newly established university in Southern California, one that was working hard to acquire top notch players to help build up their football program. Davis was pumped at the possibilities in sports, as well as education, and location. He would be part of history in the making with this new football team.

Sam had created Heather's wedding dress, and it was gorgeous. The delicate v-necked bodice featured tiny white roses placed between the pearls that surrounded the neckline. As Heather walked down the aisle, she glowed with happiness, and Sam was intensely pleased that she was marrying her best friend's son. Following the bride were the bridesmaids: Eliza, Julie, Shannon and Tracy. Then, as little Emma made her entrance, sighs of delight were heard throughout the chapel. Her long curly hair fell to her shoulders, and a crown of white rosebuds sat delicately on top of her head. Scattering rose petals along the aisle, she made her way to the smiling bride and groom. Claire's mother gasped over the precious sight of her granddaughter, who was taking her assignment very seriously, and Aunt Betty poked Uncle Richard in the ribs, making sure he saw the little angel pass by. The wedding vows were sealed with a lengthy kiss, then the bride's bouquet was thrown overhead, with Eliza the lucky recipient, a self-satisfied look covering her face.

Hours later, Claire sat in her soft cushioned chair, rubbing her feet. She looked down, grimacing at the impossibly high heels she had worn, that were now forcing her to pay the price. It had been a tiring day–a beautiful day–but a very lengthy one, and, happily, at long last, the children were all asleep, even her teenagers. The newlyweds, by this time, would be on a plane to Hawaii, paid for by Robert. She checked her watch–midnight–then glanced at the phone. After hesitating for only a moment, she picked up the receiver, and dialed Robert's number.

Two rings, with no answer. What was she thinking? He would be asleep with Shelly. She began shaking with resentment as she moved to hang the phone back up, but then she heard his voice, "Hello, hello."

"Robert, sorry to call so late; I didn't even think about the time."

His deep voice, which still, to this day, gave her chills, replied, "I was hoping you'd call, Claire. In fact, I was sitting here in my living room, waiting, and dozed off."

"I . . . I just wanted to thank you for giving us this wedding. We filmed it, Robert; I'll send you a copy. And I appreciated you letting George take your place." She didn't want to cry; dang it, why was she crying?

"Claire, I wanted you to have a worry-free day. The best thing I could give you was the freedom of being you, without fretting over me being at your side." By now, Claire was laboring to breathe. "Just like I told you in Coronado, I still love you, and always will, in my own egoistic way." She couldn't say the words she knew he wanted to hear, so just kept still, and waited. It seemed like forever before Robert spoke again. "Get some rest, Claire, and give my kids a hug. Will you please do that much for me?"

"Yes, Robert, I will give them a hug. Goodnight."

"I love–" Claire quickly hung up, not wanting to hear the last of his words.

Eliza was relieved to detect her mother talking on the phone; her preoccupation with the call would make it easier for the unruly girl to slip away, and meet Bennie Jonas. She had been sneaking out, all month, to their rendezvous on the group home's back porch, but the weather was warmer now, so they could meet somewhere more private. Tonight they would go to the downtown park. Eliza's friends thought she was crazy, and she agreed; she was crazy in love with this guy. He was nineteen, and so smart about life. He wanted to take her away, and marry her. Wow, how cool was that!

Claire turned restlessly in her bed; she must be overtired from the wedding. Glancing at the clock, she noted that it was four a.m., and realized that she had been dozing, on and off, since midnight. Every time she drifted away, she had the same dream. George and Ethel were out in the back yard, where George was pushing Emma, back and forth, in the tire swing. He was smiling a beautiful smile at the child, and Ethel was clapping her hands together, saying, "We love you, our little angel." What was troubling to Claire was that they were both dressed in white.

She mulled over her dream as she walked toward the kitchen for a glass of water. Entering the hallway, she was puzzled by the cool breeze she felt there, thinking that there wasn't a wind, that night, strong enough to blow the door open. Well, maybe she didn't shut it tightly before going to bed. She slammed the door, and pushed on it, for extra measure, then turned the lock. Padding back to her room, she climbed again into her solitary four-poster, hoping that her dream would not return.

CHAPTER 26

The CLOSED sign rocked back and forth in the window as Claire switched it over from OPEN. Sam and Claire continued to work diligently into the evening, preparing the fall classes for the Quilt Shop's open house in September. The summer business had increased, due to the crocheting class taught by their new, and highly valued employee, Clara Epperson.

Now that business hours were over, there would be no interruptions from their priceless clients, who had considerably more questions than the two women sometimes had answers for. On those occasions when Claire hadn't had all the solutions, she had ended up doing some detailed research in order to appease her clientele.

"What do you think, Sam, about putting together a booklet that would answer most of the questions we are repeatedly asked. That way, if we are measuring fabric, and other customers are trying to worm themselves up to the front, to get an opinion, we can just hand them a little booklet. If that doesn't have the answer, then I'll ring a bell for you to come up front!"

Sam pulled a face at Claire. "And how many bell ringings are you allowed? I have an instant vision of me leaving my class to run up front, responding to ninety-two rings."

"Hah, gotcha, Sam. How about, when they sign up for class, they will get one free booklet?"

Sam smiled, "Yeah, that works, and I'm also going to put together a 'Tools to Start' packet. Our customers can purchase this at the time they sign up for the Basic Piecing Class. That way, they will have all the tools, right from the get-go, and it will be at a better price than buying each item separately."

"What notions were you considering? I want to make sure I have them on the order list."

Sam approached the notion board, and sounded off the items to Claire: "Scissors (the best), rotary cutter and mat, fabric pen, long pins, beeswax, machine needles, size nine, a quilter's ruler, and lots of patience."

"What company makes patience? I want a truck load, ASAP!"

"You have more patience than I do, Claire. I'm about at my wits' end!"

"You, my soft spoken, low maintenance, uncomplaining friend, are having a melt down?"

"Yeah, go figure."

"What's going on, Sam?"

"I think it's time I told you my deepest, darkest secret. You might want to grab a bottle of whiskey on this one."

"I don't drink, remember? Neither one of us does, but I will grab a Coke!" They both dropped to the floor behind the measuring table, so that anyone walking by the shop wouldn't see them. "Okay, shoot; I'm all ears."

"Claire, the reason we are always moving is because my husband is a womanizer!"

"What! No way!"

"Yes, way. He has such a wondering eye, he seems to pluck them off a tree wherever we go, and then, when they get too serious, he runs. It took me years to figure out his habits, but, as soon as I did, I started following him. The last three moves have been as a result of his innocent, and some not so innocent, women finding out about his conniving ways. I'm sure you're wondering how come I've stayed with him. Well, if I leave, there is no way I can support my children. We'll end up in a homeless shelter, because he's told me that, if I try to leave him, he will fade away into the sunset, where he'll never be found. I'm sticking it out until the kids are on their own. Tracy is fifteen, and that means I have three years left with the bum. I've been hiding money away for when that day comes."

Claire sat with her mouth wide open throughout the entire telling of Sam's story. "Sam, please don't stay with him. Come live with us; anywhere but where you are."

"Claire, I've thought this through for years. I have a plan, and I'm not going to burden anyone with my problems. When I walk, I'm going to walk without fear, and with my head up high. The children aren't presently threatened, or in any danger, and he's very attentive to me when they are in the vicinity. It's at night when he makes it known, that he will never willingly let me go. I have put my foot down, and told him, under no circumstances, will I ever move again. I love it here, and you're the very best friend I've ever had in my life. I won't leave!"

"Is he thinking about leaving?"

"Not yet. He is having an affair with Audrey Spens. But, if she gets restless, and wants to take the next step, then he will get antsy. I hope they will be inseparable; that will buy me some time."

"He's playing hanky-panky with your boss's sister?"

"Yup. So, Claire, what do you think of your slug of a friend now?"

"I think she's an angel, and I love her more now than I did an hour ago. Come here, ya silly girl, and give me a hug, even though my tears are running into my dripping nose. Whatever you want me to do, Sam, I'm here for you, and the minute you call me, I will literally be by your side in a flicker of a second. Deal?"

"Deal," was the soft reply.

George hadn't been feeling well for months now. He had gone to Doctor Burton, but was then referred to a specialist in Salt Lake, where they could continue the examinations with their state-of-the-art equipment. The small hospital in Woodland was not big enough to justify purchasing the latest and greatest testing devices..

It was only a few weeks away from Christmas. George thought he had ulcers, but wanted to enjoy the holiday with the kids, so was ignoring his symptoms for the time being. Daniel and his wife Heather were coming home, as well as Davis from Southern California. It was a day that George was looking forward to.

It was raining the next morning, as the Watsons awoke from a restless night, with little sleep. The pain was worse, and, though the forecast was for snow, George and Ethel felt comfortable taking the drive, forty miles down the canyon, into the city. He knew he needed to be checked, and, hopefully, the doctor would give him some medication that would ease his discomfort.

Claire came to their home, to make sure they had all the paperwork they needed for the new doctor. "Why don't you let me drive you down, George? I can get Clara to fill in for me."

"No, I don't want to be a burden. You got a plate full. We'll be fine."

Ethel nodded. "My heavens, Claire, we're just going to Salt Lake, not to the end of the world."

"Okay, Okay, but drive carefully, and please call be when you start for home, so I know where you are. Okay?"

"Will do." George leaned over and kissed her cheek. "It's been a good life, hasn't it, Claire? We've made a good team, and Ethel has been a good cheerleader."

"Now, don't start getting sentimental, George," Ethel responded with a little choke in her

114

throat. "Off we go. We'll see you later this afternoon, Claire. We'll call you when we leave Salt Lake."

"I've made some vegetable soup for the family today, so I'll have some warming in the pot, waiting for your return home. Now off with you, and be careful."

George drove extra slowly, making sure they wouldn't be startled by some deer running across the road this early in the morning. There was talk at the Exchange Grocery Store that several people had spotted them lately, along the way, as they traveled the highway.

Just as the car topped the summit, and headed down the other side, George was struck with a horrifically sharp pain in is chest. He doubled over, trying to keep his hand on the steering wheel, and his senses about him, but he was only aware of Ethel screaming, and trying to help.

On the ten o'clock nightly news, the reporter told of the tragic accident on Highway Forty, where an elderly gentleman and his wife were instantly killed, as they drove across the center line, and into the oncoming diesel truck that demolished their car. George and Ethel Watson were pronounced dead at the scene of the accident.

Claire sat curled in a ball, a blanket over her shoulders. This day was a day from hell. Her children had been devastated when Claire had told them why the policeman was at her door, after finding her name in the wreckage. They had cried themselves to sleep, and now Claire sat numb: no feelings, no thoughts, just emptiness, and an eerie feeling of defeat. How in the world did the Lord think she could live without her beloved neighbors and friends?

Then a calmness filled her soul, as she remembered the dream, the dream she'd had over and over again: George and Ethel swinging little Emma in the tire swing, George smiling, and Ethel clapping her hands. They were dressed in white, and they were happy. "How selfish are my thoughts," Claire said quietly to herself. The Lord had let them go together, and now they were triumphant, lighthearted, and Claire's heroes.

CHAPTER 27

Four days after the accident, Martin George Watson, his wife Beth, and their two sons, Alexander, and Mitchel, flew in from New York, to settle George and Ethel's affairs. Claire had never met them in person; she'd only seen pictures, and had conversations on the phone. George and Ethel were very proud of the way their son had worked himself up to the top, now serving as one of the four CEOs of the Eastern Shell Oil Company.

As Claire waited inside the airport terminal, watching for the expected family, suddenly two handsome young men appeared, coming down the ramp. Claire could see George's image in the way they walked, with their heads tilted to one side, one of their grandfather's trademarks. They must be in their late twenties or early thirties, and walked with powerful strides, in a dignified manner. Alongside were their father and mother, whom Claire recognized from the many photographs placed around the Watson's home.

Claire welcomed them with open arms, and as they came close, Martin engaged her in a very tight, demonstrative hug. She, in turn, clung to the one person she knew shared her despair, wishing she could stay within his comforting embrace until the hurt went away. Claire felt that she would faint with emotion, and his shoulder seemed a safe place to land, a place where she could release her inner pain, even in an airport.

Martin felt like he was holding his dad's little angel. He knew how much his parents loved this woman and her children. They had given his dad a reason to wake up in the morning, and Martin was thankful for that.

Claire reluctantly weakened her hold around Martin's shoulders, and he looked down into her teary eyes. "Ya okay, Kiddo?"

"Oh, man," she said, her shaky laugh interlaced with remnants of her weeping, "you sound just like your dad."

They made their way to the baggage claim, then to the limo Claire had previously rented. The hour long drive to Woodland was full of bonding with a family that, thanks to George, Claire already felt a part of. She was surprised at how much George and Ethel had shared with Martin about her and her household.

Claire had booked a suite for Martin and his family at the Ashton Resort, just outside of Woodland, which catered to the needs of clientele with fame and status. As the limo pulled up, and they disembarked, the bell boy retrieved their luggage, while Martin made arrangements with Claire to meet at his parents' home later in the afternoon, after they had freshened up. At that time they would go over the living trust. Claire graciously agreed, and the bell boy called for her car to be brought around to the front entrance. As she drove back to her home, in her mind she carefully sorted through the next day's agenda.

The funeral was set for Thursday, December 1, 1988, the arrangements having previously been made by Claire, as per Martin's instructions by long distance telephone. He had read to her a letter left by his parents, detailing their wishes concerning funeral plans. As he was repeating their words, he suddenly stopped, mid-sentence. Claire waited, wondering over his hesitation. Then Martin said, "That's weird. This request is not for them individually; it's a funeral outlined for the two of them. They must have had a premonition that they would die together."

Claire gasped, remembering her dream. "Martin," she murmured, "I have something very sacred I want to share with you." Then, as Claire relayed the details of her vision, she could feel Martin's reverent awe on the other end of the line.

Robert had flown in the day before, on the same flight as Davis, both coming from California. For the next few days he would be staying at the Marriott, close to Daniel's new home in Salt Lake. He felt it would be a good opportunity to spend some private hours with his children, to let them vent, and bond with him. It would also give Claire the time she needed to finish preparations for the funeral. He was right, and she was grateful. On the Saturday following the funeral, he would move to the Ashton Resort, to be closer to the family. Shortly after his plane landed at the Salt Lake Airport, he drove a rental car to Woodland, to pick up the younger children; even Emma wanted to go with him.

Walking next door, Claire turned the key in the lock of her neighbor's house, shaking convulsively. Even though she knew that they were happy, and together, she missed them terribly. Stopping just inside the door, she took a deep breath, and surveyed the home's familiar surroundings, now strangely bereft of those who had given it life. From behind, someone's strong hands came to rest firmly on her shoulders. "They loved you so much, Claire. I can never thank you enough for letting them be a part of your life, yours and your children's. She turned to look up into Martin's face, so handsome–just like his father–and so strong. He possessed all of George's most remarkable characteristics. She knew he sympathized with her, just as George had done, so many, many times in her life.

They sat on the worn, blue flowered couch in his parents' living room, and went over the living trust. It was pretty much all in order, and Martin agreed with everything, but Claire sat mesmerized by what he had read to her. George and Ethel had left the truck to the boys, but emphasized that it was pretty much Joey's. They had also opened a small savings for the children, which was to be divided among them. None of this was surprising to Claire, but then, as Martin read the last paragraph, she nearly passed out. George and Ethel had left the house and all its furnishings to her. She instantly looked at Martin. "Are you okay with that?"

"Claire, my father left me an inheritance of more than I really need. We made this will together, and we both felt like it was the right thing to do. This isn't merely a kindness from my father, it's because you gave him a reason for living. So please, be comforted by his generosity, and by my mother's wisdom, and talent, that she has passed on to your children.

Claire's eyes were so swollen from incessant crying since the accident, she couldn't believe it possible that she had more tears, but she did. "I was the luckiest person in the world, to live next door to them, and know I was never alone, no matter how bad life's story became." He put his arms around her, and there they sat, like brother and sister, grieving over their loss, but also rejoicing, knowing that George and Ethel were together, and happy.

Sam's family were extremely involved in the services. Her daughters sang the two songs that George and Ethel had requested: *Sunrise Sunset* and *You'll Never Walk Alone*, while their mother accompanied them on the piano. It was like hearing the voices of angels echoing throughout the chapel.

After the funeral, before Martin and his family flew back to New York, he assured Claire that he would be in constant touch with her, to make sure all of the papers were in order, according to his father's wishes. In the meantime, she had the house, to do with as she desired. She knew exactly what she wanted to do with it, and could hardly wait to share the news with Sam. But, right now, she felt consumed with grief, and just wanted some time to mourn. All other concerns would have to be put on the back burner until she regained some equanimity.

Eliza was a case in point. After discovering that she had been sneaking out to meet Bennie, Claire knew she absolutely had to sit down with her daughter, and have a serious talk. But she couldn't, or didn't want to, deal with that right now; she needed a few days.

Daniel and Davis would be returning to their apartments that evening. Davis had some rigid practices scheduled before their game on Saturday, so had to catch a flight back to California, and Daniel, sensing his mother's need for solitude, offered to take his four youngest siblings home with him, to stay until Sunday. Claire was inordinately proud of her older boys, and their successes, thus far, with their futures.

The house was silent without the children there, but it, nevertheless, felt good. She took a long, hot bath, with bubbles, hoping to relieve the pain in her head, caused from grieving. After dressing in slacks, and a white eyelet blouse with a v-neckline, she slipped on her flip flops, grabbed a book, and an icy cold Coke, and fell onto her overstuffed chair. Then she just sat, staring at the room, listlessly noting that the plant in the corner was dying from lack of attention.

Her eyes moved to the kids' pictures on the wall. They were hung according to age, with a heavy shelf nailed to the wall beneath, presenting a tidy appearance, except that two of the pictures were slanted, and hanging at an angle. She sighed, feeling too lazy to get up and adjust them. Then, with another sigh, she realized she wasn't sure how to relax. Her life had been so crazy, she didn't know how to do nothing at all. She punched the cushion, hoping it would fluff it up a bit, then took a sip of Coke, and listened. Nothing. Absolutely no sounds, except for the humming of the fridge. What was she going to do all evening, alone?

When the doorbell rang, she nearly jumped out of her skin. She stood, and the sound of her flip flops, flapping against the hardwood, echoed her way to the door. She couldn't imagine who would be visiting this late at night, but when she turned the lock and opened the door, there stood Robert. "Are you going to let me in? It's cold out here."

She stood in shock. This was not a good thing, him standing there; she was too vulnerable right now. Nevertheless, she turned the latch, and opened the screen door, smelling his cologne as he passed by her, and into the living room. She continued to gawk at him. This guy was so gutsy!

"Is it okay if I sit?"

"Oh, sorry, yes. Sit, wherever you like."

"Must we be so formal, Claire?"

"Well, now that you bring it up, I was looking forward to a quiet night so I could rest, and clear my thoughts, and," she started to lose control, "it's just so quiet, and my mind won't stop remembering everything I've ever done, day by day. I think I'm losing it, and why would I even want to tell you, of all people. Why are you here? Can't I have my own private melt down?"

"Claire, come here. Please let me hold you."

"What would Shelly say, if she knew you were here?"

"I haven't been with Shelly for months; she left me for a much younger guy, and very handsome, as well. Claire, I'm a jerk. I've admitted that to George, and anyone else who'd listen, but I can't change the past. I just pay for it every day of my life. Will you please just let me hold you, and give you comfort. Nothing more, Claire. Just let me be here for you."

Claire walked toward him, and reached out her hand. "Promise, nothing more?"

"I promise." Standing, he took her hand, and led her into the bedroom, where she lay, fully dressed, on the bed, with Robert by her side. He wrapped one arm around her, while his other cradled her head. It was like he was holding a fragile baby doll. Before they drifted off to sleep, he pulled the handmade quilt up and over the two of them. Claire sighed. She needed to be held. She needed, she wanted, to catch her breath, and retrieve the sensations of being loved, and cherished, just for one night. Robert leaned over, and they gently kissed. It was soft, not demanding, and the only one throughout the night.

Claire's mind was a bit muzzy the next morning, as she awoke from a much needed night of unbroken, peaceful slumber. Then, suddenly, it hit her. Robert! She instantly recalled falling asleep in his arms, after a soft, tingling kiss. Turning toward what had, at one time, been his side of the bed, her eyes blinked at the empty pillow there, and as she pulled it toward her in a cuddle, she breathed in the smell of his cologne, lingering on the pillow case. Then she noticed a note.

Dearest Claire,

When I opened my eyes, and felt you still in my arms, I was so at peace.

I love you, Claire, and I will keep loving you forever.

As you read these words, I will be on a flight back to Colorado.

I have left my heart behind, hoping you will hold onto it. I love you, my darling Claire. Please trust me. Please let us be together again. We can move our family to Colorado and have a new start. I'll be waiting for your call.

Love always,

Robert

CHAPTER 28

After two months of mourning over George and Ethel's death, and notwithstanding the probability of some lonely years ahead, Claire's family was finally able to surge forward. Claire still picked up the phone, now and then, to call George for help, before slowly putting the receiver back with a soft click, as a fresh tear touched her cheek. Their family Christmas had been a little more quiet, a little more humble, and a little less cheerful. They had all looked forward to the new year, and now the calendar boasted February 1989.

Claire opened her dresser drawer, and pulled out some clean clothes for the day. Once dressed, she stood before the bathroom mirror, brushing through her hair, deep in thought. She had never called Robert back after the night that he had held her, and soothed her grief. She couldn't. In the few lines he had written, he had destroyed everything she had worked so hard to gain.

Did he really believe that she would be willing to pull up stakes, and take a chance on him again? Deep in her heart she didn't trust him. She wanted to, but couldn't. There were still too many "what-if"s.

It was Monday, Claire's day off from the Quilt Shop, and Eliza, now a rebellious Junior, had stayed home sick. Joey and Julie were at school, and Emma was just beginning preschool. Claire thought she would have a meltdown, when she took her youngest child to the door of the Kiddie-Kollege, but Emma, with her bouncy curls and cute little pink dress and white pinafore, responded well to the teacher, and was excited about the chance to play with the other children. Not knowing whether to be happy or sad, Claire just shrugged her shoulders, turned, and left.

When she returned home, Eliza was in the bathroom, kneeling over the commode, retching, and crying, at the same time. Claire dropped to the floor by her side. "What is it, Eliza?" She then grabbed a towel from the rack above her, and wiped her daughter's face, as if she were a five-year-old. "Tell me, Eliza, do I need to take you to the doctor? Are you in pain? Talk to me!"

"I'm pregnant, Mom," she blurted. "Just leave me alone. Okay, Mom? Leave me alone."

Claire was stunned. She knew Eliza was as wild as the wind, and she had sat down and talked to her many times, hoping she was listening. Well, evidently, her words had fallen on deaf ears. Claire's voice quivered, *"You're pregnant?"*

"Yes, Mother, and Bennie wants to marry me."

"But, Eliza, where will you live? What about school? How is he going to support you?" Claire kept rambling on at Eliza, as they continued to sit on the bathroom floor.

"Shut up! I don't want to hear all of your lectures, Mother. I hate you! Do you hear me? I hate you!"

Claire sat for a moment in stony silence. Then she slowly stood, and reached her hands down to help pull Eliza up from the floor. In a very quiet voice she murmured, "I know you haven't loved me for a long time, Eliza, but I didn't think you hated me."

Eliza was still trembling, but managed to explain how Claire had ruined her life, by letting her father leave. "If you would have tried harder," she sobbed, "he wouldn't have left us. And now he's offered, over and over, to make amends, and you still won't give in. You're so selfish, Mother, and I hate you for that." Claire's insides were quaking, but she was not going to let her daughter know how bruised she was by her coldness.

With Eliza so determined to make Claire the fall guy for all of the problems in her little world, how, in a million years, could Claire explain to her the actual events that had lead to the divorce? "Okay, Eliza, I'm not going to argue, not with you in this condition. There are things between your father and me that you will never know or understand. If you feel like you want to put the blame on me, then so be it. But, right now, let's talk about you. What are you thinking, and where's Bennie? Does he know you are pregnant?"

"Yes, Mother, he knows. We were going to run away together, but, now that I'm pregnant, we want to be married."

"And then what?"

"Mother (she spat out the word as if it caused a rotten taste in her mouth), all I want from you is your consent to my marrying Bennie. All I want is a signed paper. I don't want you at the wedding; I don't want you in my baby's life. I want to get as far away from you as I can."

Claire felt like she had just had an encounter with the Wicked Witch of the West. Who was this girl sitting next to her, with such hatred toward her mother? Where had that mother gone so wrong? That was a laughable thought; evidently it wasn't "when" she had failed, it was "that" she had. She had been unsuccessful, in every way, at being a mother to this child, at least, the type of mother who, in her daughter's eyes, fit the desired profile.

In view of Eliza's bitterness and determination, what Claire needed to do, now, was submit to this angry, distraught daughter's wishes, and simply bow out. Claire knew that this was a cross she would bear for many years to come, a cross that would remind her, every day, that she had messed up in her role as a parent to this child.

Over the next few days, Claire stood back, and watched her daughter pack her belongings, while constantly on the phone with Bennie, making their plans. Claire signed the papers, giving Eliza the right to marry Bennie Jonas, whoever this person was. She had no clue. Her daughter hammered into Claire's mind that, if she tried to stop them, she would run, so Claire regretfully stood out of her way. Eliza's siblings begged her to stay, and rethink her choices, but she simply looked at them and said, "You just don't realize how much I love Bennie. Someday you'll understand."

She hugged Joey, Julie, and little Emma, and said her farewells. Then she called her two older brothers, and told them goodbye. Even though their voices expressed dismay, she wouldn't listen. She never said a word to Claire, just picked up her suitcase, and walked down the driveway to the waiting car. A tall, handsome, black boy climbed from the beat up old Ford, and took her suitcase, then held her in his arms, and kissed her, before opening her door. As Eliza glanced back at the house, she could see her mother standing at the window, but turned her head away from the strained face, and smiled at Bennie, as they drove away.

CHAPTER 29

Claire held the paper work in her hands, signed, sealed and delivered. Everything was now legal, and George and Ethel's home was hers. The process had been lengthier than Claire had presumed, and it was always difficult for her to keep a secret, especially from her best friend.

Claire's heart was still very tender concerning the episode with her oldest daughter. After she had watched Eliza drive away with Bennie that day, she had just melted to the floor in a clump, filtering through every little thing she thought she had done right, and all the many things she had evidently done wrong with Eliza. She knew that she had been gone lengthy periods of time, trying to get the Quilt Shop up and running, but, with Emma coming, and all the chaos of trying to survive without Robert, what choice had there been? The whole scenario had been a wipe out for her, as well as her family.

She'd known she was beating herself up pretty well, two punches to the right, now to the left. "You're a poor excuse for a mother! How could you just let your daughter walk away? You're a spineless wuss!" The mental beating had continued until she'd heard, "Mommy, is it fun sitting on the floor?" She'd looked up into Emma's little face, and the thought had raced through her mind, "How many more of my children will I fail?"

The ringing of the phone startled Claire back to the present. It had been about two months since Eliza had left, so, with some concern, she picked up the receiver, and listened, thinking, at first, that another disaster had occurred. Then her troubled face became relaxed, as the conversation converted her tenseness into a warm-heartedness.

The caller was her son Daniel; he had located Bennie and Eliza in Ogden, about forty miles north of Salt Lake. He'd had them come to his home, where he'd talked to them both, for hours, trying to put some common sense into their heads. Living in a shelter was not going to cut it, not for *his* sister! He later talked to his father, and Robert, upon Daniel's request, secured an

125

apartment in Salt Lake for Eliza and her new hubby. It was a mansion, compared to the one room they had at the shelter.

As Daniel and Heather had sat in their living room, facing the young couple, he'd also asked to see the marriage license, which Eliza carried with her. He understood that his sister must be head over heels for this guy, to live the way she was, just to be with him. But, what was really driving him crazy was the well-being of the baby.

This story, as Daniel related it, just kept getting better. Claire pulled up a stool, and sat, while her son kept talking, nonstop. "I asked them how they were going to care for the baby, Mom, and had she even been to the doctor's." Heather had sensed that the answer didn't sit well with Daniel, so had suggested he get the couple some ice water, while he collected his thoughts, so that the emotions that were building up inside of him didn't turn into anger.

"Smart wife," thought Claire.

"Well, bottom line, Mom, is this: I told Bennie I wanted to talk to him, man to man. He was more than willing to do whatever it would take, to keep Eliza and the baby safe. He was grateful for any help, and promised to be a good provider, if given the opportunity. I think I like the guy, Mom. I believe he hasn't been given direction or opportunity in his life. So I hired him to work at the plant. That way I know who, and what he is, and I can help him become a stable provider for Eliza and the baby. Dad sent me some money to get them started with groceries, baby items, and such, and Heather is going to get Eliza to a doctor that she knows through her internship at the hospital. All is well, Mom." Daniel then broke down. "She's safe, Mom, and Heather and I will watch over them."

Claire was still sitting on the stool, but was now rocking back and forth, clutching the phone ever so tightly. Her words were broken with gasps, "Thank you, Daniel, thank you."

"Mom, this is the hard part: you're the punching bag for all of her anger. She needs to work out all of her inner demons, and that's going to take some time, so I'll be the go-between. Okay, Mom?"

"Whatever you want from me, Daniel, please let me know."

"Right now, I need ya, to keep praying for miracles, Mom."

That Saturday was a zoo at the Quilt Shop. They were bombarded with customers coming to pick up their free "block of the month" fabric pieces, and sign up for the "Sock Hop All Nighter" quilt classes, which would take place during spring break. Clara had an unbelievable display, showcasing her crocheted shawls, and different trim patterns for bibs, and flannel blankets. Her sign-up sheet was cleverly placed right next to the large flowered plate stacked high with her homemade brownies, each one wrapped, and ready to take, upon sign-up.

It was nine-thirty at night before Claire and Sam could turn the closed sign, like they had, so many times before. But tonight Claire had a surprise for her friend. Sam was counting the money from the day's business, and cautiously placing it into the bank bag for a drop off, as Claire pulled up a stool next to the register and cutting board. "How're things going at home, Sam?"

"You don't want to know; it will ruin our day."

"Our day is over, so let's just ruin the night. Okay?"

"Well it's not good, Claire. I think hubby is up against a wall again, and needs to run, or make a choice."

"Why don't you make the choice, Sam? Why don't you make the big, huge choice to walk out on him, and take your children, to boot?"

"What've you been drinking, Claire? Did someone put something into your Coke?"

"Yes, they did: a dose of love, and a rescue plan, all tied together, and delivered."

"What in the world are you talking about, Claire? Is this a guessing game? Because I'm too tired to play."

"You're not only tired; you're a grump!"

"Okay, I'm a grump. What else is new?"

Claire slid off the stool, and bent down to retrieve her purse from under the cutting table. She carefully opened it, humming a tune she was making up, and taking her time, enticing her friend.

"What'r'ya hiding? Chocolate?" Sam asked, as she leaned over Claire's shoulder.

"Something better than chocolate," Claire sang. "I am the proud owner of the Watson home. Furnished, may I add, and may I add, it is right next door to me, and may I add the words: here is the key." She opened Sam's hand, and placed the slightly tarnished item into her palm, folding her fingers around it, and squeezing tight.

"What are you suggesting, Claire?"

"I'm giving you the opportunity to get back some self-respect, Sam. The house is paid for, the rent is free, it's totally furnished, plus you'll be safe."

"Are you kidding me?"

"Would I kid a friend?"

Sam took hold of Claire's hands, as they jumped up and down together, screaming, laughing, dancing, and then running, as fast as they could, to the bathroom. The bouncing, along with the Coke, and having too many children, didn't help their bladders.

Not many days later Sam began living a dream. She awoke alone in her bed, then showered, and freshened up before it all began. It was a great morning; she was moving. She was leaving, and the children were coming with her. There was sunshine coming up over the hill, as well as into her heart.

Sam had bravely told–not asked, but told–Paul that she was leaving, and she was taking the girls. He tried to pull the bully act on her, but she stood her ground–because she could–and he backed down, like the coward that he was.

As Joey and Claire climbed into the renowned old truck that George and the boys had restored, her heart quickened, recalling the day he had taken her sons to see their projected undertaking. After being restored, and used by two older brothers, the truck had been tucked away for the intervening years, until now, when Claire sat behind the wheel, with Joey at her side. He was giving her directions on how to shift gears without grinding them, and whatever other instructions he felt necessary, to save his truck from being abused by his mother. Joey was the man of the house now, and he took his obligation very seriously. With the secret grooming he'd received from his brothers, he could have driven the truck better than his mom, but, instead, he affectionately and patiently taught her that it's better to drive around each rut in the road, rather than hit them. Joey was also proud that he was part of helping one special individual, and her cute daughters (the only two of Sam's offspring now remaining at home), reach their new destination.

After pulling up to the house, Joey and Claire helped Sam and her children load their personal belongings. Sam felt the sun's rays shining down on her, and noted the smiles on Shannon's and Tracy's faces as they sat on a box that was purposely placed directly under the back window of the truck. Sam squeezed in next to Joey, who in turn put his arm around his mother to make room for her best friend, whose appealing daughters were peeping in through the back window, with grins from ear to ear, as they drove away.

Claire hit every rut in the dirt road as they continued on to the main highway, which would take Sam and her two girls to their last home. They would never have to move again! As she bounced up and down with the jostling truck, Claire leaned forward enough to glance around

Joey, and see Sam's face. "Are you okay, Girlfriend?" she asked with a caring voice.

The reply was a quivering, "Yes. I never thought this day would come."

"Well, it has, thanks to George. God bless his soul, and Ethel's. Oh, by the way." Claire squirmed back into the seat, extending her foot as far as she could to push in the clutch, so they could roll to a gentle halt at the stop sign. "Have you given any thought to how you're getting to work?"

Sam chuckled. "Walking won't bother me a bit. In fact, it would be an honor to walk up the sidewalk to Main Street, and then toward the Quilt Shop, because I'm free now; I'm my own person!"

"Well," Claire drew out the word. "If you choose to walk that's great, but there is a car in the garage at your new home. It was Ethel's, and comes with the house. We just need to transfer it into your name. So, let me know when you're tired of walking," she chuckled. "I don't want to mess with your new freedom."

Sam smiled. Oh, how she loved her friend. Life was good.

CHAPTER 30

Minutes became hours, hours became days, and days turned into seasons, each one tiptoeing by, each year altering Claire's life. The thoughts she mulled over daily included the acknowledgment that life was far from being without difficulty. There was no guarantee that, as she started each new twenty-four hours, they wouldn't be the last hours of her life. After losing George and Ethel in one day, she realized the value of sunrises and sunsets, and earnestly tried not to squander away even a moment of whatever time was allotted her.

Sam, who was now her neighbor, had a few chickens in George's old coop. She was avid about fresh eggs, and how great it was to go to the nests and gather them. Claire thought, "Give me a break; it's easier to pick them up at the store," and was instantly annoyed, each sunrise, when she heard the strutting rooster's cock-a-doodle-doo. She was sure he did it just to aggravate her, but she didn't share her negative thoughts with Sam. Nevertheless, it would seem that Mr. Rooster was wiser than she. So, with new resolve, she started getting up the minute she heard him crow, giving herself more hours in her day to do the extra things she'd been in the habit of ignoring.

In spite of her new awareness, it seemed that, no matter how much she forged forward, she ended up taking two steps back. She still had her junky days, which she called *mellow yellow*: days that took all of her strength to get through. She had a mental list of some of those days: Eliza leaving–that would always be at the top of her long list; Robert's deceptions, and yet his tender touch; the day she lost her neighbors; lengthy, lonely nights, filled with the yearning to be loved, and the ache she felt from her failures. These days she just felt blah and wimpy, unworthy of the label "Mother." Thank heavens her mellow yellow days were few, especially now that she was working with Mr. Rooster on being cheerful early in the morning.

Claire's life held enough humor to keep her going, and she loved laughing at herself, and even

130

conversing with herself. For instance, when her Levi's wouldn't button–due to the ice cream binge the night before, as she watched a romantic movie–instead of bemoaning her lack of self-control, she would pat her tummy, and chuckle, "Okay, Old Girl, it's Weight Watchers for you . . . tomorrow," knowing full well that, as far as actually signing up, tomorrow would never come! Claire also had a habit of talking aloud as she cleaned, and was sometimes caught by Emma, who would look around the room and say "Mommy, who you talkin' to?"

Then there were the evening walks, when she and Sam played *if I could be Queen for a Day.* Now that was a hoot! They would look at the houses they passed on various streets, pretending to be the woman inside, and making up news reports about their day. Some stories were funnier than others, but the two friends always had a good laugh. One time Sam said to Claire, "I bet those women are looking out their windows, and wishing they could be outside, walking, laughing, and making memories with their best friend. She then turned to Claire and, in unison, they reached high slapping hands, and gave each other a "high-five."

But her biggest reality was when she lay in her bed at the end of the day, and took time to evaluate the hours she had just lived, wondering if she'd made a difference, or if she'd just slid through, unnoticed. Then, in the quiet of the night, she would punch the pillow, over and over, to get comfortable, knowing that, no matter how many times she tossed about, trying to still her thoughts, or how many restless turns she made, trying to fall asleep, it wouldn't change her world.

The frequency of her walks with Sam was dependent upon class schedules at the Quilt Shop, but usually they could venture out on weekends, plus two nights during the week. As the two of them turned a corner, during one of their late-night strolls, the full moon was peeking over the Rocky Mountains, giving them an "aha" moment. What a beautiful evening! They could hear the crickets in the fields out by the pond, and the barking of a few dogs, who gave warning of their passing.

Claire's voice was breathless, as she asked Sam how Greg and Paul were doing in the military, but Sam, who was a zealous walker, didn't gasp at all as she responded, "They are doing extremely well. Greg is stationed in Washington, and Paul's in Texas. I'm so proud of both of them. Paul actually wants to make it a career, and Greg is still debating. Have you heard how Eliza is doing?"

"The last report I received from Daniel was that all is going pretty well. You know she is tending our grandchildren, right?"

"Yes that's what Heather told me, and she's doing a great job."

Claire smiled. "Who would have believed that we would be grandmas to twin boys! It just seems so dreamlike when I think of them, and how handsome they are. It's obvious they took after their grandmas. Right, Sam?"

"Yeah, right, Claire. Sorry to disappoint you, but they look like their father, to the 'T.' But, may I add, their father is very handsome!" She smiled at Claire. "Heather gives me weekly reports, too, but she doesn't get into a lot of details about Eliza. I think she and Daniel have made some huge positive changes with regard to Eliza's and Bennie's future. I can't imagine where the two of them would be if it weren't for the intervention, can you?"

"No, Sam. Eliza's top priority, four years ago, was to get away from me, and her life as she knew it, as fast as she could go. Thank heavens Daniel and Heather found them. I wouldn't even know what Eliza's little girl looked like, if it weren't for Heather mailing me the pictures. I'll always have gratitude in my heart for Heather calling me, and letting me know when Eliza was having the baby. Unbeknownst to my rebellious daughter and her husband, I drove down to the Ogden Hospital, and saw my first grandchild. I will never, as long as I live, forget how beautiful she was, lying there all bundled up and snug. The nurse on duty was so kind, she picked her up, and brought her over to the viewing window; that was my first close look at baby 'Star.' Lots of black, curly hair, and those soft pink cheeks. And, as I was tapping on the window, talking to her, she opened her eyes, as if to say, 'Hi, Grandma.' I couldn't keep the tears from streaming down my face. I wanted so badly to hold her; I wept convulsively, and then walked away. Now she's four, and I still haven't held her."

"Claire, you never told me you went to the hospital alone."

"I know. I just wanted to be by myself that day. But, as I looked upon that beautiful baby girl, I felt the Spirit of God standing behind me, giving me the strength I needed."

Sam cleared her throat, moved by Claire's story. "Well, Friend, it's been a blessing for both of us, to be able to share our two grandsons. Right?"

"Right!"

They both stopped walking, and looked at each other, then moved together for an emotional hug, before the honking of a car horn reminded them that they were standing in the middle of the road. They immediately jumped back, landing in a ditch of cold irrigation water, not knowing whether to laugh or cry.

CHAPTER 31

Claire picked up her purse and sewing bag as she glanced at the class schedule for the night. There were nine classes offered now. "Wow!" she thought to herself, "These classes are full."

The Q-Bs (Quilting Beginners) had an impressive sign up, fifteen in all. She continued to scan down the list to see if Sam was teaching that night. The "Oldies but Goodies" class had been moved to the next week, to accommodate a couple of the women who were still on vacation. This was a tight group that had started when the Quilt Shop first opened, and, with them, it was all or nothing. Last year all fifteen of them went to Sisters, Oregon, to attend a quilt convention. Needless to say, Sam and Claire heard a lot of interesting stories, not only about the classes they took, but about their journey: a journey of friendship. Claire stopped checking the class list as a whimsical thought touched her mind: she and Sam had also been on quite the journey, and they hadn't even left town.

The Quilt Shop now employed six women: three for the morning shift, and three covering the night shifts, their schedules depending on whether they were clerking or teaching. Claire and Sam thought it would be a good move to extend their hours to ten in the evening, in order to accommodate more classes, and give those who worked on the floor an opportunity to shop later.

Claire had now owned the business for close to ten years. It was one choice that had given her a safe place to land. Sam had been right next to her throughout the whole eventful time, and they'd gratefully leaned on each other in all situations. As the customers would say, "You can't have one without the other."

"Hey, Sam," Claire gave a shout, hoping Sam could hear her in the back room. A few customers jerked in surprise, and Claire thought to herself, "Oops."

Sam's head peered out from the class room. "Yes, my mild, dignified friend, can I help you?"

"Yes, you can. I was wondering if you could go walking tonight. I checked the schedule, and you have no classes."

"Well, my little queen bee, thanks for doing that. I'm an empty nester now, so my time is pretty much free time, while you, My Lady, still have two children to dote over. Will Julie and Emma be okay?"

"Oh, yeah, I forgot. I have children. Let me look at my planner. Actually Julie has Young Women's at the church, so I will see if Emma wants to play with Sarah next door. I'll call Sarah's mother; I'm sure it will work out. So let's just plan to leave our doors at 5:30 p.m."

"Gottcha, Girlfriend. Hey, let's walk down by the creek in the north fields so we can pick some cattails. Then, on our way back, we'll turn where the stream turns, and go up by the abandoned house where Nielson's used to live. The autumn trees are beautiful there; we can stop and pick a few leaves to go with our cattails."

"My word, Sam, do I need to bring a wagon?"

"Yeah, that would be great, Claire, and you can pull me in it after I have accumulated all that I can possibly hold. What a super idea; I haven't been pulled in a wagon for a very long time."

"Oh, give me a break, Sam. My heart is busting from your whining. But, if you trust me to pull you, I would be happy to accommodate your wishes. That is, if the wagon will hold you!"

As their conversation unraveled, a couple of the customers stared at them, and another one boldly said, "Enough, already, you and your yapping! I'm trying to concentrate on my pattern."

Claire immediately lowered her voice, and stage whispered to Sam, "Now see what you've done? You got us in trouble."

Sam's mouth dropped open as she pointed to herself, saying quietly, but firmly, "Me! No, *you* got us in trouble." She smiled, and waved. "See you later?" Claire, who was still holding her sewing bag and purse, tiptoed out the door; she knew if she stayed any longer her customers would throw her out. In a nice way, of course.

At five-thirty, sharp, they both appeared through their front doors, and met on the sidewalk, dressed for a hike: stretch pants, baggy shirts, and walking shoes. Sam wore a cap, but Claire hated the feel of anything on her head. She had her hair pulled up into a pony tail that flipped back and forth with each step. Sam's baseball cap was one of her son's; she always looked so cutesy, no matter what she wore.

"Well, are you ready to hit the road?" she asked, as if she were Claire's coach!

"I'm ready, but I might be lagging behind you, Miss Sprinter, because someone I know wanted to make sure I brought a wagon."

"Claire, you're so thoughtful and endearing; that's why I love you so. Now, let's hit the road; we have a lot to do before the sun sets."

The walk was a little slower than usual, due to the wagon, but it was such a beautiful evening, they didn't mind the easier pace. As they made their way toward the north fields, they could hear the birds chirping, and frogs croaking. Nearby, a magpie squawked, worried that someone was invading his territory. As they traversed the lower fields, some parts of the road turned into dirt paths, which would became very dusty if a car were to drive by. But, so far, it was just Sam and Claire, out doing their thing.

Claire stood at the edge of the creek, while Sam ventured to a place where she could reach out and cut the cattails. She almost slipped a few times, but Claire squealed, to let her know that she was losing her balance.

"Would you stop yelling, Claire? It makes me think there is a snake or something."

"There *is* a snake, Sam! Look over there!"

"Oh, my word, that's just a little water snake; he's not going to hurt anyone."

"Yeah, easy for you to say, but they give me the creeps!"

"I think I have enough for us to make a beautiful arrangement for the Quilt Shop. Now let's go get the autumn leaves."

"I'm with ya on that; give me your hand, and I'll help steady you." But Sam looked at Claire with a blank stare. "Sam, I said, 'give me your hand, so I can help you back up onto the path.'"

Sam continued to stare at Claire, still clutching the cattails. "Who are you?"

"Oh, that's funny, Sam. You're standing in water with snakes, and you don't know who I am!" But then Claire noticed the vacant look on her friend's face. "Sam, stand still; I will come toward you. Stay right there, Sam, I'm–" Sam toppled into Claire's arms, and they both fell into the marsh. Claire was no longer worried about the snakes; she was trying to maintain her tenuous hold on her friend. "Sam! Sam! Wake up! What are you doing? You're scaring me!"

Claire started screaming, and crying. "We are out in the fields; I don't know how to help you!" Then Claire looked up to the heavens, and said out loud, "Dear God, please help me get my friend some help. Please help me. Please, I need help!"

Claire felt strength come into her arms, as she pulled Sam to the wagon, and laid her down the best she could. Sam's feet dragged on the ground, as Claire pulled the wagon to the road,

135

hysterically screaming, "What is happening? Stay with me, Sam. Please, don't leave me Sam. Please–"

Just then a rusty old truck came around the bend, out of nowhere, a cloud of dust following behind. Two older men jumped out, leaving the doors wide open. "What has happened?" the taller one yelled.

Claire was sobbing. "I don't know. My friend just passed out. She's breathing, but I can't get her to wake up."

As the two men lifted Sam, the cattails which she had clung to all the time that Claire was dragging her to the wagon, finally fell from her hand. The shorter man jumped up into the bed of the truck, and spread out some horse blankets, then reached down to retrieve Sam from the other man's arms. Claire climbed into the back, and dropped to the blanket, so that Sam could be laid down, with her head resting in Claire's lap. Claire gasped for air; she couldn't breathe for crying.

"Now, Missy, we are headed to the hospital, and I want you to hold her as still as you possibly can. Da ya hear?"

"Yes, I hear. Just hurry!"

"We'll go as fast as old Betsy will take us."

Claire rocked back and forth, back and forth, murmuring the words, "Please, don't leave me, Sam. Please don't leave me."

A few minutes later–which, to Claire, seemed like forever–they pulled up to the Valley View Emergency Door. After that, everything was a blur. Claire gave them all the information she could: what had happened, and where family members were located. She hadn't known any phone numbers, but luckily Sam had, in her pocket, a piece of paper on which were penciled her brother's name and number. That was unusual, that she would bring that along.

Claire sat in the hall for what seemed to be hours before the doctor came out from the examination room. "Claire, we are sending her to St. Marks, in Salt Lake. She seems to have some pressure on her brain, and we need to get her to a specialist. We've contacted Edward, her brother, and he will be meeting the ambulance there with her mother. The best thing for you to do is go home and get some rest. Edward said he will call you as soon as they know anything."

Claire lowered her head, and agreed that she needed to go home. "Doctor Burton, before I go, I need to thank the two gentleman who helped us get here. Do you know where they are?"

"Just a minute, and let me ask the staff."

136

Doctor Burton soon returned, and put his hand gently on Claire's shoulder. "Claire, Stan helped put Sam on the gurney, and he said the two men left after they knew that you were in good hands, but they wanted to make sure you got this message: "They heard your prayer.""

CHAPTER 32

Doctor Burton prescribed a sedative for Claire to take when she got home. Then Carol, one of the nurses who had helped deliver all of Claire's babies, approached, asked what had happened, and how she could assist. She had noticed Claire in the waiting room, looking stunned, and talking to the doctor.

Doctor Burton filled her in, and then asked if she could drive Claire home. Carol could see that Claire was in shock. "Sure thing, Doctor Burton. Come on, Claire, let's get you home, and into your nice comfy bed. You'll feel better after you get some rest."

Claire looked at Carol and murmured, "I feel like I'm broken; my heart is broken." Carol took Claire's hand, and with her arm around her shoulder, lifted her up, and walked her to the car. There was silence between them as Carol drove the short distance to Claire's home. Julie had returned from her church activity, and had picked up Emma from the neighbors. They were sitting at the large kitchen table that claimed its place within the curve of the bay window, through which they could see all of the activity in the neighborhood. Julie watched as a strange car drove up. She then gently pulled the sheer curtain back to see who was inside, but couldn't make out its occupants. She looked at Emma as she stood. "Stay right here, Emma, and finish your snack. I will be right back."

"Okay, Sissy. Is it Mommy?"

"I'm not sure, Sweetie, but stay here, okay?"

"Okay."

Julie opened the back door that led out to the driveway, then stood with her mouth open as she watched Carol help Claire out of the car. She had never seen her mother look so hollow. No smile, no twinkle in her big blue eyes, and no spark in her walk. "What's happened to my mom?" she screamed. "Is she okay?"

Carol looked directly at Julie, and with calmness, but direct words, guidance came out of her mouth. "Julie, your Mom has had a horrific experience; she is in shock. I need you to go and turn her bed down. We will get her settled, and then I'll talk to you, and we'll figure out where to go from there. Where is Emma?"

"She's in the kitchen, having a snack."

"Okay, as soon as you turn down the bed, go sit with her, and keep her occupied, while I take care of your mother. Also," she added, "what is your oldest brother's name?"

"Daniel."

"Daniel, that's right. I was trying to remember all of your names, since I was the one who helped deliver all of you," she chuckled, lightening up the situation.

Julie immediately did as she was told, then quietly pointed the way to Claire's bedroom, and asked, "Do you want me to call Daniel?"

"Yes, that would be a good idea. Keep him on the line for a few minutes."

Carol guided Claire to her bed, and continued talking as she filled a class full of water from the bathroom tap, and opened the small package of pills. Claire heard Carol tell her to undress, and put her nightgown on, and crawl into bed, but she felt like she was in a tunnel or a fog. Yes, that was it: a fog, and pretty soon she would see the sunlight, and she and Sam could finish picking the autumn leaves. Where was the wagon? She needed to put the leaves into the wagon!

Claire felt the sunlight as it filtered in through her bedroom window. She needed to get up, but she couldn't even remember going to bed, let alone losing hours of her life. Then she fell back on the pillow as her mind replayed the previous evening's episode. Was this a bad dream? Did last night really happen?

Hearing voices, she pulled herself up, and carefully walked out to the kitchen, where sat Daniel, Heather, Julie and Emma. Daniel stood, and walked toward her, with Heather a footstep behind. He opened his arms and folded her inside; then Heather took his place, a river of tears flowing as reality set in.

Claire looked at her daughter-in-law. "How is Sam?"

"Mom had surgery last night, Claire; they found a tumor. It's not good; it's terminal." They held each other, sobbing, neither one wanting to let go. Daniel surrounded them both with his arms, his truehearted comfort sensed by the two women in his life.

Claire subsequently tried to get back to some kind of a normal routine, but she didn't know

139

what normal was anymore. She moved, she slept, she ate little, she went through the motions of working, listening to all of her caring customers express their sympathy. Then, in the evening, when she arrived home, she always put on a happy face for Julie and Emma, even though she was exhausted by the smallest tasks.

She took the time to visit Sam at her brother Edward's home in Salt Lake, in spite of the fact that her friend didn't know her. Claire pretended that she did, and would hold her, rocking back and forth, humming, or reminding Sam about all their adventures. Sam just loved being held, but looked at Claire like she was a stranger. Nevertheless, Claire felt in her heart that, at some level, Sam knew it was she. Despite the way it tore her up each time she visited, she persevered, knowing that Sam would definitely be upset with her if she didn't.

Claire had no one to talk to any more, no one to laugh with, no one to cry with, no one to walk with, no one who would listen to her babbling. *She wanted her friend back; oh, how she wanted her friend back.* Sam owned half of her heart, and Claire didn't know how to live with just a half.

As the months passed, Sam's brother conveyed to Claire that the doctors couldn't believe she was still surviving. He commented that she was a zombie, but they loved her minute by minute, feeling sure that she wanted to leave this world.

Claire thought very hard and long about his words. Sam was a little stubborn when it came to some things. "Well," Claire said to herself, "my friend is a *big* stubborn, not a little." She smiled to herself. "Gottcha on that one, Sam." As Claire pondered the situation, she felt Sam trying to speak to her, even though they were miles apart. "What is it, Sam? What do I need to do for you, so you can go home?"

Suddenly Claire's memory was jarred by a few words Sam had spoken when they were having one of their girl nights. *"Before I die, I want to make sure all five of my children have a pieced quilt, made by me, so I can cover them with my love as they sleep."*

Claire immediately walked across the yard, and unlocked Sam's door to what used to be the Watson home. Going on a scavenger hunt, she found her answer in the bedroom closet: four quilts, beautifully hand pieced and quilted, with one of the Parker children's names pinned to each masterpiece. Claire fell to her knees, and pulled out a box tucked away in a back corner. There, on top, was the last child's name: Tracy. Gently lifting the lid, she peered inside, and discovered the blocks, very carefully stacked, waiting to be sewn together. Claire broke down, and as the tears slipped down her cheek, she realized that she needed to finish what her dearest friend had started, so Sam could meet the angels who were waiting for her.

Later, as the sun slipped behind the mountains, leaving an orange glow in the sky, Claire gently carried the box in through the door of the Quilt Shop. She felt a reverence as she turned to face the radiant sunset. "I hear ya, Friend. You want to go home, and I will help you get there."

Tears had become a perpetual part of Claire's face, but she disregarded them as she approached the "Oldies but Goodies" sewing group, who were already visiting, and sharing quilt squares. The room fell quiet as Claire walked in, with her moist face and forced smile.

"I have a favor to ask you sweet women." She proceeded to share the story of Sam's "Before I Die" list, letting them know what was in the box, and asking if they would be willing to help Sam go home to her Father in Heaven. Needless to say, there was not a dry eye in the classroom as they all stood in unison to look in the box.

Nelda took the lead, and declared an all-nighters service project. Within minutes assignments were made, and the sewing machines were humming. Judy, who was working the evening shift, organized, and provided guidance in the placing of the blocks. The women were driven by an angelic atmosphere, and it seemed to Claire that Sam was watching over them, making sure the stitches were straight.

The first all-nighter was a success–the quilt top was sewn together–so they planned another gathering for the next night. The sign on the Quilt Shop was turned to "Closed," as the ladies adjusted the room for a quilt frame, their continuous jabbering filling the air with bliss. Sandwiches were ordered in, but "no charge" was written on the tag from the Crown Café, once they were informed, by word of mouth, what these ladies were doing. Claire felt like they were stitching a pathway to heaven for Sam. On the third day the quilt was finished, and the women's faces were damp from tears, their fingers cramped from stitching. But they had completed the gift of love, on behalf of a dear friend.

CHAPTER 33

Daniel and Heather came to pick up Julie and Emma for the weekend, and, when Claire told them about Sam's quilt, they were both awed at what had transpired within a few days. Claire agreed that it was something of a miracle. Still, though gratified by the service she had performed, she was empty inside, and thought it unfair that her young daughters should be forced to watch their mother regressing on a daily basis. She wasn't the same mom, the one they loved and felt safe with; she was just a woman forcing herself to live, so that her friend could die.

Claire stood in the doorway, waving goodbye, not knowing, anymore, how to feel anything. There was an enormous nothingness in her life, a boulder that was blocking her senses. It was all she could do, just to breathe. She picked up the quilt, and drew the curtains back in her living room, so she could have the sun's rays, not only to warm up the space, but to give her the light she needed to bind Sam's quilt.

Scissors, needle, thread: she was ready. A voice tinkled in her head, "You should really have an icy Coke while you stitch, Claire. You always have a cold Coke to sip when you sew." Claire immediately recognized the voice.

"Okay, Okay," she answered aloud, as she made her way to the fridge to snatch the drink. "You're so bossy, Sam. But, if it makes you happy, I will fix me a cold icy Coke, with a squirt of lemon. Will that make you happy?"

"No, but it will make you happy, you grouch."

"What? You're calling me a grouch? The nerve! I'm working on your quilt, and you're calling me names."

Claire could hear Sam's laughter, and then, with the fading of the sound, her whispered, "I miss you so much."

"Okay," Claire said to herself, as she took a deep breath, and settled back down to her task.

"Here is my Coke, my needle, my thread, my scissors, the quilt, and the sun beaming in to keep me warm. Now, my dear one, each stitch will bind this quilt, but will also bind our memories: one, by one, by one."

Claire worked well into the evening, until she took the last stitch, and sighed, moving her cramped fingers back and forth, then knotting, and clipping the thread. "Done," she whispered, folding the quilt neatly. She was tired; she had sat without moving for hours on end, to the point of exhaustion, but hadn't wanted to stop. Her head plunked backward, easing into the padded back of her chair. She closed her eyelids, and whispered to herself, "I just need to rest my eyes."

Suddenly she was surrounded by a light so bright it seemed to pierce her eyelids, giving her a visual sensation. She blinked, trying to focus on the scene before her, as she clutched the quilt tightly; wanting to make sure she hadn't shifted the fabric in any way. She had made each fold with a loving touch, and it had to be perfect. It was the last gift of love she would be able to offer her friend. Claire quickly glanced down at the quilt, giving her eyes relief from the brightness that engulfed her.

Then, raising her head, she saw a soft path leading off into the distance. She was aware of a figure at its end, but was first captivated by the beauty of the flowers which spread out on each side of her: hundreds of flowers, dancing on a rich green hill. Then her eyes focused upon the image at the end of the path: a woman sitting on what almost appeared to be a throne of beautiful rock. As the woman stood, and started walking toward her, a tear tiptoed down Claire's cheek. Sam! Oh how beautiful she was. She was smiling, and there was a twinkle in her eye.

With each gentle step she came closer, until she stood directly in front of her friend. Claire looked lovingly at the vision before her, and whispered, "Your quilt is finished."

Sam's smile was radiant, exquisite. "Thank you, Claire. I want you to know I'm okay. I'm happy. I've been blessed in many ways, and you are one of my dearest blessings. Thank you for being my friend. I love you.

"Now go and be happy, Claire. This is not a sad day; this is a good day. We will always be friends. Saying goodbye should be a beginning, not an ending; we need to say goodbye, so we can move on.

"It's so wonderful here, my friend, and I will be anticipating the day we will see each other again." Sam put her arms around Claire, and kissed her check, then softly turned and walked away with the quilt.

143

The phone was persistent in its continued ringing, and Claire tried to place her whereabouts as the sound echoed in her head. She stood slowly, realizing what she had just experienced, then picked up the phone, and slowly moved it toward her ear. It was Heather, and she was crying; then Daniel took the receiver. "Mom, are you there? Mom, I have to tell–"

"Daniel, you don't need to tell me. I was with her, Daniel. I was with Sam when she died. I was able to say goodbye."

Claire needed sleep; she was exhausted. She went to her room and lay on her bed, yearning for oblivion. Within an hour, or maybe two, she felt a warmth by her side, and a strong arm surrounding her. She thought she was dreaming, but also sensed her quilt being tucked inwards, and felt the comfort of its stitches.

Her eyes flickered as they gradually came into focus, and she realized it was Robert lying by her side, holding her, comforting her, loving her. Soft music played in the background, soothing her heart, aiding in its healing. She started to speak, but Robert put his finger to her lips, and hushed her with a soft voice. "I'm here, Claire, because I care. You need me here, and I need to be the one to give you comfort. We'll worry about tomorrow when it comes."

She closed her eyes; she wasn't alone. For this moment in her life she needed Robert, once again, to just hold her close. "When someone puts their arms around you, life isn't so cold and cruel," she thought, "because they are taking some of the pain away: the pain that is so hard to bear alone.

CHAPTER 34

Robert stayed with Claire until Sam's funeral was over. He had never remarried, and wanted Claire to come with him now, telling her that there was nothing holding her to Woodland anymore. But she couldn't imagine sharing her life again with Robert. When, and if, she did leave, she wanted to sell the Quilt Shop, and move to Holladay, where she would be closer to her grandchildren.

Then Robert proposed a different plan. During the time he had spent there, throughout Sam's funeral and burial, he and his daughters, Julie and Emma, had had some deep soul searching talks. They loved their dad, and he wanted to be with them as much as possible. Davis was still in Southern California, beginning a career in sports medicine, and Robert's job had landed him permanently in San Diego, where Joey was attending college. Robert thought it would be great to have Julie and Emma come live with him, where they could enjoy the ocean, the weather, and endless new opportunities. He had talked to the girls, and they were pumped to think they could possibly entertain such an idea, but all of their planning needed Mom's approval.

Sixteen-year-old Julie promised that they would continue to be the good girls that they already were, but Claire worried about Emma getting homesick; after all she was only ten. Emma looked at Claire, and hugged her as she whispered, "It's okay, Mom. I'll love you forever, no matter where I live. And, if I get homesick, I'll come visit!" She acted like she was twenty instead of ten. Claire wasn't going to stand in their way. It would be beneficial for them to live with their dad; he would be a good father to them.

Even though everyone was off to a new adventure, for the most part her family was still connected. They were not only siblings, they were devoted friends, united by caring hearts and souls.

"Claire," Robert said in parting, "if you ever change your mind about us, I'm only a phone call away."

Claire wouldn't cry her last tear. She knew there would be many more to come. But she needed to heal, and didn't want to be a burden to her children in the process. As Robert and the two girls boarded their plane, she stood waving; she'd refused to say goodbye. But then she could hear Sam's words whispering in her ears, "Saying goodbye is just another beginning."

The more Claire thought about it, the more she realized that Robert was right. There was nothing in Woodland, now, to keep her there. Her children were gone, and the Quilt Shop was no longer the sanctuary it once was, when Sam had been a part of it. It was time, again, to say goodbye.

CHAPTER 35 – 1994

Claire swiped a hand across her sodden cheeks, placed the "Sparkling Stars" quilt squares back inside her sewing basket, and carried the now cold pizza to the garbage. Tomorrow she would begin packing for her move to Holladay. "Well, Sam," she said aloud, "I've sold the Quilt Shop, and am getting ready to start another new adventure. I wish you were going with me, dear friend." She then smiled to herself, acknowledging the fact that, no matter where she went, Sam would always be there by her side.

Years passed, and life seemed to move along; hearts were healed, and dreams became reality. Following the move to Holladay, Claire's life became peaceful–lonely at times, and very quiet– but with serenity in her heart. She had done all she could do as a mother. She wasn't perfect, but she tried every day to be the best she could be, in service, as well as love for her family.

One bright morning she was on her hands and knees in front of her Holladay home, weeding around the rose bush she had planted in Sam's memory, and reminiscing about her friend's love of roses, and the fact that her middle name was even Rose. They used to laugh about Sam being a beautiful, fragrant rose, while Claire was the thorns.

As she squatted there, tugging at the weeds, she heard a car drive up, but gave it little thought, supposing that it was pulling in next door. A few minutes later two sets of black patent leather shoes appeared before her on her grass. Claire adjusted her position, and looked up. There stood a couple of the cutest black girls she had ever seen. She then felt two hands behind her, lifting her from the ground. Turning, she discovered that the hands belonged to Eliza, and realized that the two beautiful girls were her own granddaughters. "Star," she whispered, as the taller girl smiled, and stepped forward to hug her grandma, their tears blending. Claire never wanted to let go.

"Mom," Eliza said, "I want you to meet Becky. And little Bennie is due in three months." They all gathered in a circle, feeling triumph in their embrace. Claire knew there was no need for questions. It was a "lets-just-be-a-family-again" hug.

Suddenly a little Shitzu puppy ran up to them, and jumped on Becky, wanting to be picked up.

"Dolly, come here! Here, Dolly; here, Dolly." A nice looking, older gentleman came running around the corner, trying to catch the runaway puppy. "Oh, sorry to interrupt you ladies, but my pup got away from me. I just moved here from San Diego, and she's still trying to find her way around. My name is Charlie, and you ladies are–?"

Eliza introduced her daughters, and then put her hand on Claire's shoulder, saying with a grin, "This is my mom, Claire. She's single. What about you, Charlie?"

Claire gasped at Eliza's forward remarks, but Charlie only smiled. "Yes, I'm a widower, but I have a son who lives here. By the way, I love chocolate chip cookies; can your mother make good cookies?"

Eliza smiled, "Yes, that is one thing I love about my mother, and miss to this day: her chocolate chip cookies."

Claire could hear the conversation going back and forth, but she was concentrating more on the prayer she was whispering to God.

The End

Acknowledgments

Throughout my lifetime I have been blessed with many, many friends, all of whom have played a gigantic role in my life. They have been with me when I needed someone to lean on, laugh with, cry with, travel with, complain with, eat chocolate with, pray with, and say goodbye with. Friends are like angels; they appear out of nowhere. Recently one of those friends was a beautiful person named Nannette. Her love for books gave me the courage to continue writing, and finish what I had started seventeen years ago. She offered to edit my manuscript, and I have been able to fly on the wings of an angel. Thank you, Nannette, for your strong wings!

About the Author

Billie Jo Spanton Maurer grew up in the little town of Heber City, Utah, where she graduated from Wasatch High School in 1965. She has, from her first marriage, four sons and four daughters, who have blessed her with twenty-one grandchildren. She now resides in Clinton, Utah, and is married to Charles Maurer, her retired Navy man, who always has a story to tell. BJ (as she now prefers to be called) loves to sew and piece together quilts (she calls herself a "piece maker"), feeling that the fabrics bring warmth to her heart. During the 70's she owned two fabric stores, and still maintains her love of textiles, and finds joy in choosing just the right designs for her next project.